Fairies of Titania Book 1

The Last Fairy Door

N. A. DAVENPORT

This is a work of fiction. All the characters and events portrayed in this book are either products of the author's imagination or are used fictitiously. Published in Norfolk, VA

ISBN: 978-1-7338595-6-1

www.nadavenport.com

Library of Congress Control Number: 2020905335

For Madeline

A book is magic you can carry wherever you go.

CONTENTS

CHAPTER ONE

The long stretch of highway seemed to last forever. Amy watched out of the window from the back seat of her grandmother's car as they passed thin belts of trees, long rows of fences, and acres upon acres of farmland. Golden fields of wheat and neat rows of fruit trees cast long aisles that flashed before Amy's eyes as the car sped over the highway.

Overhead, the pale-blue sky reached from horizon to horizon, only broken by a few scattered puffy clouds.

"We're almost to the house, dear," Grandma Kerry soothed from the front seat—for the tenth time.

Amy sighed and continued staring out the window.

She hadn't been complaining. In fact, she had barely said a word since her grandmother picked her up from the airport. She'd obediently followed her grandmother to the parking lot and buckled herself into her seat. She'd shrugged noncommittally when Grandma Kerry asked how her flight had gone, and she shook her head when asked if she was hungry—the flight attendants had given her a meal already.

But Amy's grandmother seemed determined to keep up a conversation, even if it was one-sided.

Amy continued to stare out her window and only answered questions when absolutely necessary as Grandma Kerry drove them out to her farmhouse in the middle of nowhere.

It wasn't that Amy disliked her grandmother. The old lady seemed to be kind, and if anyone understood what Amy was going through, she did. It was just that Amy didn't want any of this to be happening. It shouldn't be happening.

Amy was supposed to be at her own house, where she could see the ocean outside her bedroom window. She should be near her own friends and her own school. And, most of all, Amy's father was supposed to be coming straight home to her from whatever music recording he was doing.

Only he hadn't. He'd stopped to visit Grandma Kerry, his mother, on the way home and had fallen ill. Before he could catch his next flight out, he was so sick that he had to get checked into the hospital. Now Amy had to move in with her grandmother until he got better. If he ever got better at all.

When her father left on his trip, he had told Amy that he'd be home by the end of the week. Now people were whispering that he might never come home again.

A tear trickled down Amy's cheek. She sniffed.

"Oh, sweetheart, don't you worry," Grandma Kerry soothed. "We'll get you settled at the house and go visit your daddy first thing tomorrow, okay?"

"Okay," Amy whispered, wiping her cheeks.

Amy could see the peaked roof of a white farmhouse coming into view over the top of the gentle hill ahead of them. It was a perfectly square building surrounded by a small grove of wide-branched trees that swayed gently in the wind.

Wide fields surrounded the house and trees, one full of tall grass and fenced off from animals, another occupied by a small herd of brown cows, flicking their tails against fat black flies.

The car slowed and turned onto a dirt road, kicking up a cloud of dust as it bumped and bounced its way up to the house.

When they got nearer, Amy noticed vegetable and flower gardens on the left side of the house. Down the other side of the hill, in the distance, there was an old grey barn with holes in its roof and its door hanging awkwardly on its hinges.

The car came to a stop in the middle of a cloud of dust, and Grandma Kerry turned off the engine.

"The upstairs bedroom is all yours," she announced. "That room used to be your daddy's when he was a little boy, you know." Grandma Kerry smiled as she tucked her keys into her purse.

Amy nodded silently, unbuckled her seatbelt, and opened her door, sliding out onto the dusty driveway in front of the farmhouse.

The house looked a lot bigger now that she was standing right in front of it. It was three stories tall, was shining white, and had a covered porch that wrapped all the way around it.

"Make yourself at home, honey. Do you want some water? Or lemonade? I'll bet you're thirsty after that long drive."

Amy shook her head and stood still. The strange house made her feel nervous.

Her grandma smiled sadly at her. "It's okay, sweetie. Take your time. The bathroom is the first door on the left if you need it. I'll get started on some food for you. Come on in when you're ready."

Grandma Kerry took Amy's suitcase and walked into the house, leaving the door open for her.

Amy took a deep breath and looked around to explore her new surroundings more closely. Clusters of flowering bushes grew around the front steps boasting bright pink, purple, and white blossoms. Some of the trees surrounding the house were heavy with fruit. Amy noticed plump golden apples and velvety purple plums.

She decided to walk around the house to see what was around the corner and found a fenced-off chicken coop sheltered by small trees. The hens were clucking happily as they pecked away at the grass and weeds. One of them had a cluster of fuzzy yellow chicks trailing after it. Amy couldn't help but smile and reach out, hoping a chick would let her pick it up, but they skittered away as soon as her hand came near them.

Amy drew her hand back with a small sigh and walked around to the other side of the house. Here, she found an open field filled with waist-high grass. It smelled like warm sunshine, and, as the breeze rushed over the stalks, the whole field moved like shining green and gold waves.

Down in the distance, Amy saw the old, broken-down barn. It was half-covered in bushes and vines. To the right of the barn stood a beautiful tree with bright orange berries.

Amy bit her lower lip curiously as she stared at the old barn. What could be in there? If she went to explore it, would she find old horseshoes? A family of foxes? Hidden treasure?

"Are you about ready for dinner, dear? I've made us some sandwiches," Grandma Kerry called from the house.

"Yes, I'm coming," she answered.

As she looked away to return to the house, a little flicker of movement caught Amy's attention from the direction of the barn.

She looked back. Was there some animal wandering around down there?

Then she saw it again, only this time there was no mistaking it. There was a person out there exploring the old barn already, and that person was much too small to be an adult. It was another kid like her! Were there other children living nearby? And if so, why was this one on her grandmother's property?

Amy frowned and narrowed her eyes at the distant figure, trying to see more clearly. Whoever it was climbed the side of the barn and crawled in through the broken window, disappearing from view. The kid didn't come back out.

Amy wrinkled her forehead. She must not be the only one interested in investigating the barn. She sighed and turned back to the house. She wasn't in the mood to try to make new friends, so she'd just have to wait for the mysterious visitor to go away before she could explore the creepy old barn for herself.

In Grandma Kerry's kitchen, Amy slid into her chair as her grandmother placed a plate of food in front of her on the table.

"Grandma," she began, hesitantly, "do any other kids live nearby?"

"Oh, no, dear. I'm afraid not. The Sheffields have a grandson who comes to visit now and then. I think he's . . . oh, about fifteen now. But don't you worry. I'll be bringing you to church on Sundays and there are a few girls your age there. And we can sign you up for dance or gymnastics or whatever you like in town. You'll be able to make lots of new friends here."

Amy frowned at her sandwich. This was not what she'd been thinking at all. First, the fact that her grandma seemed to presume that Amy would be living here forever put a lump in her stomach that erased her hunger completely. And second, she did not want to make new friends. Her old friends at her old house were just fine, thank you very much. Her grandmother kept bringing it up, as if having friends would make it okay that her father was in the hospital and getting worse. No new friends were going to be able to replace *him*.

Her grandmother said a quick prayer and they quietly ate their ham sandwiches together in the brightly lit kitchen. Amy only took a few bites of her sandwich before giving up and picking at the crust with her eyes downcast.

When they were done eating the sun was starting to sink low toward the western horizon, turning the sky orange and the clouds shades of purple and pink.

Amy had gotten up early that morning with her Aunt Lisa to get ready for her flight. Since she'd traveled to a new time zone, she felt more tired than she should for seven o'clock in the evening. She started to yawn.

"Are you feeling ready for bed, dear?" Grandma Kerry asked, noticing the yawn. "I've already put your luggage in your room for you. And the upstairs bathroom is ready for you to take a shower after your long trip."

"Okay," Amy said, nodding sleepily.

She climbed the carpeted stairs to the second floor. It was warmer upstairs; the summer heat collected in the rooms, barely affected by the slight breeze wafting in through the open windows.

She turned into the small bathroom off the upstairs hallway and rinsed off in the shower, allowing the water to cool her down. She felt a little better once her shower was done and she slipped into her cotton pajamas. She went to the room that used to belong to her father and lay on top of the covers on the little bed.

After a few minutes, her hair and skin had dried and the cooling effect was lost. Grumbling, Amy climbed back out of bed and turned on the light. The bedroom window was only halfway open. If she could only open it wider, maybe some of the cool night air would blow in.

She gripped the bottom of the window with both hands and pulled up, but the window didn't budge. She yanked it up as hard as she could, grunting with the effort, and managed to get it to squeak and groan upwards a few more inches.

Amy blew out a frustrated huff and leaned against the windowsill to let the cooler outside air blow against her face.

Her window looked out onto the open field. The expanse of uncut grass looked silvery-white in the moonlight. The gentle night wind blew across it in waves.

In the distance, down the hill, the old barn stood dark and deserted, like a solitary ship on a magical sea.

As Amy sat there gazing out her window, a sudden flash of golden light came from the barn. It illuminated the building from within, bursting from the broken window, the holes in the roof, and the cracks between the boards.

Amy lifted her head and stared at the barn curiously.

Could it be that the kid she'd seen climbing into the barn earlier was still there? Maybe whoever it was had a flashlight or camera.

There was a knock at the door. Amy turned to see her grandmother come in with a soft smile on her face.

"I noticed your light was still on. Is everything all right?"

"Oh, um, it's just hot. I was trying to open the window."

Grandma Kerry nodded. "Yes, it has been rather warm this past week. Here, maybe this will help."

She opened the closet, which was packed with boxes and blankets and folders and even an old sewing machine, and pulled out a big square fan.

"I'll just get this set up in the window for you—whoops!" As she was swinging the fan away from the closet, she accidentally backed into the low bookshelf against the wall and knocked over a pile of books and a few other random items.

Amy hurried over to pick them up and stacked them back on the shelf.

"Thank you, dear. I'd forgotten how warm this room gets in the evening, being on the western side of the house. The fan should have you all cooled off in no time. You know, when your father used to sleep in here, he got so used to having the fan on in the summer that he couldn't sleep without it on in the winter." She chuckled, setting the fan on the windowsill.

Amy wasn't paying attention. She sat on the floor holding a small, velvety blue box with fancy silver lettering on top. She'd stopped before placing it back up on the bookshelf because of what the lettering said.

In beautiful sweeping handwriting, written in ink that looked like liquid starlight, the top of the box had one word written on it.

Amaryllis.

CHAPTER TWO

Amy frowned, puzzled, and turned the package sideways, squinting at the shiny writing. Why did this box have her name on it . . . the fancy, long, weird name that her parents had given her when she was born?

Amy never went by Amaryllis. The first thing she always had to do when she started school or visited a new doctor or dentist was correct the adults so they would call her *Amy* instead of the name written on her file.

"Grandma, what's this?" she finally asked, holding up the box so her grandmother could see.

Grandma Kerry turned to look at her, then kneeled down and slid her glasses up her nose to examine the box.

"Oh, I'm sure I don't know, dear." She took the velvety blue package in her hands and ran her fingers over the silver lettering. "It does seem to have your name on it, doesn't it?"

Amy nodded.

"To be honest, the writing looks like something your mother might have done. She had the most beautiful penmanship."

Amy's eyes flashed from the box to her grandmother's face. "My mother?"

Grandma Kerry smiled sadly. "Yes. She spent a good deal of time here before she married your father. But that was before you were born."

Amy took a breath and turned her attention back to the blue box. Could her mother have left it here? For her?

She knew very little about her mother. Her father always kept his comments about her vague, and it seemed to pain him to remember her too much.

Amy knew that her father had met her and married her a few years before Amy was born. She'd helped her father with his music, writing songs and lyrics with him. Whenever anyone asked Amy where she got her beautiful red hair from, her father answered that it came from her mother.

Amy's mother had left mysteriously when Amy was

only a few months old. Amy had overheard a lot of different speculations from adults about why she left and where she'd gone—everything from *she didn't want the responsibility of having a child* to *she got mixed up with the wrong crowd and had to skip town.*

Amy didn't believe any of the theories because her father didn't believe them. But no matter how hard she tried, she still couldn't believe the one thing her father told her repeatedly and often, that Amy's mother had loved her dearly.

If her mother had loved her so much, then how could she have just left like that? No word. No note. She hadn't even taken the car or any luggage, or so Amy had heard through all the gossip. So it was a shock to see something from her mother, here at her grandmother's house of all places, with her name on it.

"Would you like to open it?" Grandma Kerry asked. "By all accounts, it seems to be meant for you. Maybe she was holding on to it for you, to give it to you when you were born."

Amy nodded, not taking her eyes off the box.

Grandma Kerry tugged at the lid, pulling the top open slowly. "Of course, it might just be a onesie or a bib," she murmured.

When the top came away and revealed what was

inside, they both saw that the sparkling item was definitely not meant for a baby.

A milky-white oval pendant sat in a bed of shimmering silver silk. The pendant had an image etched into the smooth stone that looked like a tree with wide-splayed branches above and, mirroring the branches, a mass of roots reaching out below. An ornate bail, that looked like vines twisted around a smooth leaf, held the pendant to a long golden chain.

"Well, what do you know?" Grandma Kerry said. "I believe this was your mother's necklace, or it's one very much like it. I never saw her without it around her neck."

Amy reached out her fingers to touch the pendant. Something about it seemed to draw her in.

"Go on, dear. This is obviously meant for you." Grandma Kerry held the box out closer to Amy, and she picked up the pendant with trembling fingers.

The stone felt cool and weighty, but there was something about it that seemed to tingle against her fingertips and make her whole body feel a bit lighter, like she'd been carrying an invisible burden her whole life and only now noticed it because it was gone.

"Wow," she whispered.

"It is very beautiful, isn't it? I always did admire this necklace."

Amy nodded as she slipped the chain over her head and smiled at the shimmering golden sparkles.

"What was my mother like?" Amy asked without looking up.

"Your mother? Oh, she was very lovely. But surely your father has told you that. You do take after her."

Amy nodded. "He says I have her hair and eyes."

"Yes. She was gentle and kind, but she also loved to laugh, and she pulled the most hilarious pranks."

"Really?"

"Once she replaced all our framed family photos with pictures of cows. We didn't even notice until a visitor came and pointed it out." She laughed. "And she had the most beautiful voice, too. She could practically sing the birds right out of the trees."

Amy smiled. "Like in a fairytale, right?"

"Right. Your father always did call her his fairy princess. And she certainly was enchanting."

"I wish I could have met her," Amy confessed, looking down at her pendant.

"Yes, I wish you could have, too."

They sat in silence for a minute while the fan blew fresh night air over them.

"Well," Grandma Kerry said, sitting up straight and assuming a businesslike manner, "it seems to have cooled off in here nicely, don't you think?"

Amy tore her eyes away from the necklace to nod in agreement. The fan in the window was doing the trick. The air in the bedroom felt almost as cool as outside now.

"Then you and I had better get some shut-eye. There's a glass for water on the bathroom sink if you need it. And don't be afraid to knock on my door if you need anything else."

Amy nodded again and even managed a small smile. "Okay."

Grandma Kerry smiled at her with twinkling eyes. She stood and stepped into the hallway, turning back to wish Amy a goodnight before closing the door.

Before climbing into bed, Amy stood in front of the fan for a few more minutes, letting the current of cool air flow over her.

Outside her window, all seemed pitch black except for the distant twinkling stars and sliver of moon drifting overhead. She watched the old barn for any new activity, but nothing seemed to happen. Whatever was going on there appeared to be over for the night.

Amy crawled into the small bed and pulled a light throw-blanket over herself; it was still too warm to even consider crawling under the heavy down comforter.

Tomorrow, Grandma Kerry would be taking her to see her father at the hospital. Was he really as sick as everyone was saying? He'd seemed fine the last time Amy had seen him. She couldn't imagine how someone could go from perfectly healthy to gravely ill in a matter of weeks.

She comforted herself that he was probably getting better already. Her father was a lot stronger than people thought. Even if he was very sick, he would be better soon.

Instinctively, Amy grabbed for the pendant and held it, clasped in her hands. Its smooth coolness seemed to comfort her. It was evidence that her mother had at least thought of her at some point in the past, enough to leave a gift for her.

Amy knew she probably shouldn't wear the necklace to bed, though. The chain might get twisted or caught in her hair as she slept. She decided she would take it off soon and place it on the bedside table for the night. Not just yet, though. She would wear it a little longer.

A few minutes later, Amy's eyes fluttered closed and her breathing relaxed as she drifted to sleep.

The next morning, Amy felt as though butterflies were flitting around in her stomach while she dressed, brushed her teeth, and tried to eat some oatmeal, fruit, and cream that Grandma Kerry made for them.

She couldn't seem to hold still, swinging her legs as

she sat in her chair, fiddling with her hair and bouncing in her seat.

"Are you feeling a little nervous?" Grandma Kerry asked as they started driving down the dusty gravel road.

Amy was holding the pendant that hung from her neck, stroking the texture of the engraved tree design under her fingertips. She dropped it and looked up when her grandma spoke.

"Uh, maybe . . . a little."

Grandma Kerry smiled and placed one warm hand over Amy's. "It'll be okay. Your father will be so happy to see you. He's missed you a lot."

Amy nodded and turned away to hide her frown. She wasn't worried that her father wouldn't want to see her. Of course he wanted to see her. She was worried about seeing him! What if she got there and he really was as sick as everyone said? What if he didn't even look like himself anymore? She'd been telling herself all this time, ever since her Aunt Lisa got a phone call from him at the hospital, that he couldn't really be as sick as they said and that it would all be over very soon. Even if it was worse than the usual cold or stomach bug, he was at a hospital with doctors who knew how to take care of him. Surely he would get better soon.

But what if she got there and discovered that all these things she'd been telling herself were lies?

As she stared out her window, looking out along the grassy field to the old barn down the hill, she caught a flash of what looked like a pale face peering out at them from the dark broken window.

She blinked and it was gone.

The drive to the hospital seemed to take forever. Amy's grandmother turned on the radio to play some classical music to pass the time. It didn't work very well. Amy fought wave after wave of anxiety as she thought about where they were going. The anxiety was relieved only slightly by long stretches of boredom as she stared out at passing farms and listened to the sleepy voice of the man on the radio announcing the next piece of piano music.

Eventually, farmland gave way to houses, stores, gas stations, and restaurants, and then they were finally pulling into the parking lot at the hospital.

"We're here, honey," Grandma Kerry said.

Amy blinked out of the hypnotic stupor she'd fallen into. She stared out at the looming cream-colored building above them.

"My dad is in there?" she whispered.

"Yes, and I'm sure he'll be delighted to see you."

Amy climbed out of the car, still staring nervously at

the hospital and fiddling absently with the pendant around her neck.

"Take my hand in the parking lot, dear."

Amy obligingly reached out and took her grandmother's hand. Normally she would have complained. She was ten years old, after all. It's not like she was about to run out in front of a moving car or something. But she was too nervous to object.

Everyone was saying that he was sick, too sick to come home, but he'd been perfectly healthy the last time she'd seen him. How could that have changed so fast? How could anything have kept him from coming home to her?

Part of her wanted to believe that, as soon as they were together again, everything would somehow be okay. But another part, probably the part that actually thought about things rationally, whispered that, if he could have come home, he would have and he wouldn't be stuck here in a hospital.

Amy and her grandmother walked hand-in-hand up the walkway, between concrete pillars that held up an arched glass roof. When they reached the main entry, big sliding doors opened automatically and a rush of cool air blew into their faces, smelling like floor cleaner and medicine.

Grandma Kerry took them up the elevator to the

third floor, where Amy's father was staying. As they got closer, she could feel her heart pounding behind her ribcage. It felt like it was trying to climb its way out of her throat. She tried to swallow it back down.

The elevator opened, revealing a smooth, tiled floor that led up to big double doors with tiny windows in them. This area looked less inviting than the lobby had.

They pushed their way through the doors, and Grandma Kerry approached the counter, greeted one of the nurses, and started writing on a clipboard.

"Oh, you must be Amaryllis!" the nurse gushed, leaning over the counter. "We've heard so much about you! Wow, look at that beautiful red hair!"

"I go by Amy," Amy told her reflexively. It was usually the first thing she said to grown-ups. The ones who knew who she was usually knew her name because her father had dedicated his debut album, *For my darling daughter, Amaryllis*.

She looked around at all the doors along the hallway. Which of those rooms was her father in?

"I think that's a perfectly lovely name, Amy," the nurse said, still smiling. "I bet you're the one *Fire in Disguise* was written about, right? I just love that song!"

Amy nodded, making her red curls bounce against her shoulders. Her father had written that song for her a few years earlier. It was a nice song, but she'd quickly tired of random strangers singing it to her when they found out who she was.

“Your father will be so happy to see you. But you must remember to be gentle with him, okay?"

Amy gulped and whispered, “Okay."

“We're all signed in now,” Grandma Kerry announced. “Are you ready?" She was smiling, but the smile didn't quite seem to reach her eyes.

Amy nodded.

"Right this way," the nurse said, guiding them down to one of the doors. She knocked quietly and pushed it open. "There are a couple of visitors here to see you, Mr. Porter," she announced.

CHAPTER THREE

Amy tiptoed through the door and peeked around her grandmother to see the room.

Her father was lying on a white hospital bed with metal rails. A plastic IV tube was taped to his hand and arm, a beeping machine stood next to him, and a bag of clear fluid hung from a metal hook overhead.

Worst of all, he didn't quite look as she remembered him from a week earlier. He looked tired. His face was covered in a short prickly beard. His skin looked so pale that it seemed almost transparent. There were dark bruise-like circles under his eyes, and his breath came shallow and quick, like he couldn't breathe in all the way.

"Daddy?" she asked uncertainly, even though she knew it really was him. Part of her wanted to run to him and give him a hug, but she was also scared. Scared of the strange changes that she could see. Scared because the nurse had told her to be gentle. What if she hurt him or accidentally pulled out one of the tubes that might be keeping him alive?

"Hey there, bug. It's good to see you," he said, smiling wearily at her.

There was an awkward pause; Amy didn't know what to say next, and apparently her father didn't either. Amy shuffled her feet against the polished floor.

"How are you liking Grandma's house?" he asked.

"It's . . ." She looked up at her grandmother, who was watching her curiously, and decided to tell a little fib. How could she say that she hated every moment being at her grandmother's house? It wasn't really Grandma Kerry's fault. Amy just wanted to go home. "It's nice. I get to sleep in your old room."

His smile widened. "Did you put the fan in the window like I used to? I know it's been hot lately."

Amy did smile then. "Yeah."

Her father coughed once, winced, and laid his head back against his pillow, closing his eyes. "I used to sit in front of that fan and stare out of the window for hours."

Amy walked across the room to stand by his side, but she didn't dare touch him for fear she would interfere with something important.

"Will you get better soon?" she asked, timidly. "I want you to come home." She felt her eyes prickle, and the room around her started to look blurry. She blinked and wiped her eyes.

"I know, little bug. I know." Her father sounded sad, too. "But the doctors say I can't go anywhere right now. A car or airplane trip . . . well, it wouldn't be good for me."

Amy's chin started to tremble.

Her father opened his eyes and looked at her. "But I am so happy to see you. I missed you so much." He reached out and stroked her hair, tucking a strand behind her ear like he always used to. "And what is this?" His fingers found the gold chain around her neck and his eyes followed it to the pendant that Amy was holding in her hands. His eyes widened in amazement and flashed to Grandma Kerry.

"Is Lily . . ." he started.

Grandma Kerry shook her head. "We found that in your old bedroom. The box had Amy's name on it, so we figured it must be for her."

The machine next to her father's bed had started beeping faster. Amy looked at it worriedly.

"It's okay. I'm okay." Her father rested his head back on his pillow, squeezing his eyes shut like he was in pain. "That is a very pretty necklace. Your mother has one just like it."

"That's what Grandma Kerry said," Amy murmured.

Her father didn't answer. He started coughing again and groaned in pain.

Amy frowned and looked back at the nurse who'd walked them in. Surely someone would try to help him!

The nurse came to the bed and fiddled with some of the buttons on the machine.

"I'm sorry . . ." Her father gasped between coughs. "So sorry, sweetheart."

Amy's frown deepened. He only ever called her "sweetheart" when she was very upset, like if she fell off her bike and skinned her knee. But she wasn't the one hurting right now, he was.

Grandma Kerry walked over and put her hand on Amy's back, leading her away from the bed and out of the room. "He needs to get some rest, dear," she said in a low, choked-up voice.

She sat Amy down on a plastic chair outside of her father's room and rubbed her back soothingly.

Amy looked down at her hands and saw that they were shaking. She rubbed them together to try to get them to behave.

"Mrs. Porter, can we speak with you for a moment?" the nurse said, poking her head out of the room.

"Yes, of course." Grandma Kerry crouched down a little to meet Amy's eyes. "Just wait for me here, okay?"

Amy sniffed and nodded. Her grandmother stroked her hair once, and then she went back into the room to talk with the nurse.

Amy stared at her trembling hands.

It was true. It was all true, just like deep down she knew it would be. Only now she couldn't pretend everything was all right anymore. Her father was clearly very sick. She stifled a sob and wiped her nose on her sleeve.

Finally, she decided to find the bathroom to at least wash her face. Sitting in a chair, not doing anything, was making her feel anxious.

There was a bathroom near the entrance to the wing they were in. Amy went in and washed up slowly, taking her time so she wouldn't have to sit still in that chair any longer than absolutely necessary.

When she'd scrubbed with soap and water and carefully dried her face and hands with a paper towel, she decided she couldn't delay going back to her chair any longer.

As she was walking past the front desk, she overheard the nurses talking amongst themselves. She stopped to listen, her short frame hidden behind a stack of folders.

"The little girl is just darling, though," one of them

said. "That curly red hair and those blue eyes . . . she's almost too cute to believe."

"I know, the poor thing. They don't even live here. He said she flew in from Massachusetts to stay with her grandma. I think she just got here yesterday."

"This has got to be so hard for her."

"Yeah . . . I can't even imagine." The nurse sighed. "His fever spiked again. The antibiotics aren't as effective as we hoped."

"Then there isn't much left we can do," the first nurse said, softly. "It's times like this I wish we had some kind of magical cure-all."

They were both quiet for a minute. Amy felt like she was frozen in place. She didn't dare move. What if they started talking about her father again?

"Did you know I have all his albums on my phone?" the first nurse asked.

The second nurse chuckled. "You're such a fangirl."

"I know. It would be a sad, lonely world without Brandon Porter in it."

Amy heard the clicking of a computer keyboard. The nurses didn't say anything else. She tiptoed back to the chair by her father's room.

A few minutes later, the door opened and Amy turned to peek inside. Her grandmother was wiping tears from her eyes, and her father gestured for Amy to come over to him.

She entered the room and approached his bedside, wringing her hands nervously.

"Are . . ." She gulped. "Are you going to be okay, Daddy?"

He grimaced and looked her in the eyes. "Listen, bug. Things might get tough for you soon. They already are, I can see that. Remember what I've always told you: life isn't always going to be easy or comfortable, but you have to do the best you can for the people you love, even when it's difficult and painful."

"I know, but . . ."

He shook his head, struggling to say everything he wanted to while gasping for air. "I wish I could fix everything. But the best I can do is try to make sure you're with people who love you."

"I want to be with *you!*" She couldn't help the sob that came out then.

"I know, bug, I know." He closed his eyes and leaned his head back against his pillow, taking quick light breaths. Amy thought for a moment that he would open his eyes and start talking again, but after a minute it was clear that he'd fallen asleep.

"Come on, honey, let's let your dad rest. He's been through a lot today." Her grandmother put a hand on

Amy's shoulder to guide her out of the room, and the nurse followed them.

"You can be sure that we will do everything in our power to make Mr. Porter comfortable," the nurse said.

"Thank you," Amy's grandmother replied, shaking her hand.

When they got back to the car, Amy buckled herself in and waited until they were driving down the highway to ask a question that had been burning in her mind.

"Is he dying?"

Grandma Kerry flinched a little at the question and wiped her eyes. "That's what they think, sweetheart. They're doing everything they can for him, but nothing seems to be working."

Amy felt her face scrunch up again as her heart climbed back into her throat.

"But listen to me. Your father is one of the kindest, most generous people I've ever known. And I'm not saying that because I'm his mom." She smiled a little. "He's always been ready to help people and give whatever he can to anyone who needs it. He's already lived more than most people who live to a hundred because of his generous heart and kindness toward others. Of course he wants to stay here and be with you. He wants to watch you grow up and maybe meet his own grandchildren someday. But even if that doesn't happen, the world is already a much better place because he's been in it."

Amy looked away. She didn't want to listen. She didn't care how many other random people her father had helped with his charitable donations or made happy with his record-breaking music. He was *her* father, not theirs! He was supposed to always be there for her.

When they got back to the farmhouse, Amy's grandma brought her into the kitchen and started slicing vegetables to make a salad for lunch. She handed Amy a small knife so she could help cut up the lettuce and cucumbers. After a minute, Amy dropped the knife on the cutting board, scratching her hand furiously.

"What's the matter, dear? Did you cut yourself?"

"No, the metal knife makes me itchy. I react to some metals like that. Dad says I'm allergic."

"Allergic to metal?" Her grandmother held out Amy's hand and examined her palm. The skin that had been touching the metal handle was red and irritated. "Oh, my! Here, wash your hand, and I'll get you some cream for that."

Amy went to the sink, squirted soap on her hands, and started scrubbing.

"You know, you probably inherited that from your mother," Grandma Kerry said, pulling a tube of hydrocortisone out of her first aid kit.

"My metal allergy?"

"Yes, she barely ever touched metal things at all because she was so afraid of a reaction." She brought the cream to Amy and helped rub some of it into her palm, but her skin was already looking better.

"It doesn't bother me too much." Amy shrugged. "It's only things like steel that make me itchy. I can hold a soda can or a phone, no problem."

Her grandmother finished slicing the vegetables for the salad, and they ate lunch together in the quiet kitchen. When they were done eating, Amy helped her grandmother with chores around the farm for the rest of the day. She enjoyed feeding the chickens and watering the garden. Her grandmother even showed her how to milk the cows.

After a light dinner, Amy took a quick shower, then ambled wearily into her bedroom. The fan was already in the window, so her room was much cooler than it had been the previous night.

She slipped into her cotton nightgown and put her necklace back on, standing in front of the breeze from the fan and enjoying the cooling sensation on her neck and face.

Something moved out in the field, and Amy leaned forward to peer outside. Her pendant rapped against the windowsill, so she tucked it under her nightgown to keep it out of the way as she leaned out to investigate.

Could it have been the strange kid . . . the one who was playing around the barn before?

A gust of wind swayed the branches of the big tree by the barn and blew against the tall grass.

Amy frowned. Maybe it had only been the rustling of the grass that caught her attention.

Then something happened; she was sure of it this time. Through the broken barn window, she saw a small flash of yellow light, like the flicker of a nearly dead flashlight or a firework fizzling out.

She continued leaning forward and stared, but the barn window was completely dark now. Was it possible the kid, whoever it was, was still there, sleeping in the barn at night? Did they have a flashlight? Or were they starting a fire?

Amy had to find out.

CHAPTER FOUR

Amy crept out of her room into the dark hallway. Her grandmother had already gone to bed. There was no light coming from under her bedroom door, but Amy wasn't sure if she was actually asleep yet or not. It wasn't all that late—the sun was only just starting to go down. Still, even if Grandma Kerry heard her come out into the hallway, she would probably think that Amy was going to use the bathroom or getting a drink of water. She had no reason to suspect that Amy would sneak out.

Amy felt a small pang of guilt. Normally she wouldn't sneak around breaking the rules, but she was burning up with curiosity over what was going on in the old barn, and she needed something to distract herself from thinking about the hospital visit. And, besides, nobody had told her she wasn't allowed to leave the house or wander out into the fields, so she wasn't technically breaking any rules.

Amy quietly slipped downstairs, feeling her way with light feet down the creaking stairway.

On her way through the kitchen, she grabbed a couple of apples and tucked them into the pockets of her nightgown. She didn't know how long she would be exploring the barn, and she felt like she might want a snack after such a light dinner.

Not wanting to bother with her shoelaces, and uncertain whether the field was dry or not, she slid her bare feet into the rain boots by the door. Then she took the flashlight hanging from a hook on the wall and slipped out the door, closing it quietly behind her.

Amy waited for a moment, listening for any noises from the house that might indicate her grandmother was waking up, but the house stayed dark and quiet.

Amy peered out at the shadowy shape of the old barn down the hill, just visible against the red-orange horizon. It didn't look like anything unusual was going on there now. Had she imagined the strange flash of light?

She thought for a moment about going back inside, climbing into bed, and trying to go to sleep. She didn't want to do that . . . not yet. If she lay in bed, in the darkening room, she wouldn't go to sleep very easily. She would lie awake, remembering whose room she was sleeping in. Remembering how her father had looked when she visited him. Remembering what the nurses had said when they thought she couldn't hear. Her father wasn't getting better. It would take some kind of magical cure to help him now.

No, she wasn't ready to go back in there yet. She was already outside; she might as well check it out.

Slipping around the corner of the house so that the light wouldn't shine into her grandmother's window, Amy turned her flashlight on and marched out into the field. She pushed her way through the tall grass toward the barn. The dry stalks shone gold and faint green as they rustled and cracked in the beam from her flashlight. The sky was getting darker and, beyond the bright patch of grass in front of her, Amy could barely see anything. Stars winked above her. The wedge of the moon rose low in the sky behind as she trudged ahead, hoping that she was still going the right way.

Then she pushed away a clump of grass and nearly stumbled into the old wood of the barn wall.

Amy flashed her light right and left for a second, getting her bearings. A large broken window was set in the wall in front of her. She remembered seeing the strange kid climb through it yesterday and wondered if she could do the same, but it was too high up. Plus, she was wearing a nightgown and big clunky rain boots, and it would be awkward trying to climb anything.

The large doors leading into the barn were around the corner to her right, so she made her way along the wall toward them.

Even with her flashlight, it was difficult to see everything. She banged her shin on an old rusty plow set against the barn wall, hissed in pain, then limped around it. There was other trash, too, scattered about the barn, such as buckets, broken glass, and a couple of old rusty horseshoes.

A rat scurried away from the light when she came around the corner, and Amy froze in alarm. It seemed to be alone, though—or at least no other rats came out of hiding right away.

Amy turned the corner and examined the barn doors, wrinkling her forehead as she considered how she might get through them. One of the doors was held firmly shut by a massive growth of ivy. The other sat crooked, holding on by a single hinge. The gap between the doors wasn't quite wide enough for her to fit through, so she tucked her flashlight under her arm, gripped the wood of the crooked door, and pulled.

The wood creaked. A tiny trickle of dust floated down from somewhere above her.

Amy put the flashlight on the ground so she could get a stronger grip, then heaved with all her might.

The doors creaked again, then groaned and snapped as she widened the gap between them.

Panting and sweating, but pleased with her accomplishment, Amy picked up her flashlight and poked her head through the opening.

The inside of the barn was covered in a thick layer of dust. It smelled musty, like mold and mildew. Old broken furniture lay piled against one wall. Some sort of large farming machine with rows of rusted blades sat under the broken window she'd considered climbing through. Now she was glad she'd decided against it.

Something scurried up among the rafters. Amy pointed her flashlight in the direction of the noise. "Hello. Is anyone in here?" she called.

There was no answer. Then the scurrying came again and she caught a glimpse of a striped tail. A wedge-shaped face poked out from behind a beam of wood, peering at her with shining eyes.

"Oh, it's just a raccoon." Amy sighed, relieved.

Feeling more confident, she tucked her hair behind her ears and squeezed her way in between the doors, getting her nightgown dirty and covered in splinters in the process.

When she finally got through, she stood, brushing

her nightgown off and looking around with her flashlight.

"I wonder what the light was, though," she said to the raccoon. "Have you been trying to build fires?"

The raccoon didn't answer. It scurried farther into the hayloft as though hoping its unwelcome visitor would leave soon.

Then there came another rustle from the far side of the barn, followed by a noise like something banging into metal.

"Ow!" a boy's voice cried. It was definitely a boy and not just her imagination.

Amy jumped and backed up a few steps. "Hello?" she called. "Who are you?"

"Go away! I'm nobody. I'm not here. You're dreaming. I don't want to be your friend."

Amy scoffed. "Well, I don't want to be your friend either, Mr. Nobody-Imaginary-Dream-Person, whoever you are! Are you the one who's been trying to start a fire in here?"

"I wasn't! Ugh! Ow! I wasn't trying to start a fire! Now just go away!" His voice was tight and strained, like he was gritting his teeth in pain.

"What's wrong with you?"

"None of your business. Why don't you just go home?"

There was no way Amy was going back to the farmhouse now. Not only was this encounter infinitely more interesting than she'd been expecting, but this strange boy also seemed to think he could order her around. She was now obligated to prove that she didn't have to listen to him.

Amy purposefully walked toward the sound of his voice, smiling at the little growl of anger he made, and leaned against one of the support beams. She pulled one of the apples out of her pocket and started to casually munch on it.

"Why are you sneaking into my grandma's barn? You don't belong here. Why don't *you* go home?" she asked.

"That's none of your business either."

She took another bite of apple. It was amazing how his refusal to answer her questions was only making her more curious.

"Do you . . . have food?" he asked. There was a rustle of dry dust and dirt. It sounded like he was standing up.

"Yeah, I brought a couple of apples." She heard him take a step closer.

"The lady who lives in the farmhouse . . . she's supposed to live alone."

Amy frowned, wondering what he was getting at. She pushed away from the support beam and stepped closer. She could just make out his silhouette in the dark horse stall where he was hiding. "Well, she did live alone until yesterday. I just moved here."

The boy groaned and leaned into the wall. "Ow . . ."

"Did you fall when you climbed in here?" She looked back at the rusty metal contraption under the window. She couldn't imagine the damage that thing would do to someone who landed on it.

He sighed. "Yeah, I fell right on that horrible farm equipment. Can I have one of your apples?"

Amy took another step closer, trying to see him. "Yeah, you can have one. Come on out. What's your name? How badly are you hurt? Maybe my grandma can help. Where did you come from? Where do you live?"

There was a long pause, and then the boy sighed again. "Fine. If you feed me, I'll answer all your questions. You might not believe them, though."

The boy came out into the light, and Amy's mouth fell open when she finally saw him properly. He was dirty all over, as she'd expected him to be since he'd been hiding out in a barn, but his face was strangely beautiful, like he came from some other world filled with glorious heroes, marvelous creatures, and bold adventures. His clothes were simple, without any buttons or zippers that she could see. He seemed to have a piece of fabric tied around his waist for a belt, and around his neck was a shiny blue pendant on a woven cord. He grimaced in pain as he walked, but his legs and arms seemed to be working fine. She didn't see any blood or obvious injury on him.

The boy eyed her like he was waiting for something, and Amy remembered that she'd promised him one of her apples. She pulled the second one out of her pocket and held it out for him. "Here you go."

He took it gingerly. "Thank you." He looked at the apple and back up at her, like he was deciding whether or not to eat it.

"Aren't you hungry?"

"Yes, I am." Still, he hesitated.

Amy rolled her eyes at him. "I didn't poison it, if that's what you're thinking. I'm not the evil queen from Snow White."

He made a face, like she'd said something that made him uncomfortable, but didn't comment. Then he held the apple with two hands, bit into it, and moaned. He took another bite before he'd even finished chewing the first, greedily chomping down and stuffing as much as he could into his mouth at once. Amy thought he looked like a chipmunk eating an acorn.

When he was finished eating the apple, seeds and all, he licked the juices off his fingers and gazed at the floor like he hoped there might be pieces there to pick up and eat as well.

"Wow, I guess you really were hungry."

He nodded and brought his gaze back to her. "I'm Flax."

"Huh?"

"You asked my name. It's Flax."

"Oh . . . that's kind of a weird name."

He pulled himself up indignantly. "No, it isn't. I bet your name's weird."

Amy felt her face heat up. He'd hit closer to home than she wanted to admit. "My name's Amy, since you *didn't* ask."

"See? I told you so," Flax said, waving his hand like she'd made his point for him.

Amy narrowed her eyes at him suspiciously. She only went by Amy because it was a completely ordinary name that any girl might have. Amaryllis was much more unusual. It was a good thing she hadn't told him that name.

"Anyway, *Flax*, what are you doing here in my grandma's barn?"

He sighed. "I came to collect these for my family." He opened a small pouch that was tied to his belt and pulled out a handful of small orange berries."

"You came for the berries from our tree?"

"Yes, they're very important."

"Why?"

He grimaced like he didn't want to answer. "We use them to make a drink that we need to survive."

"Oh . . . well, that's odd. But I guess you can take them. I didn't know they were any good for eating. Hey, where do you live? Grandma said there weren't any other kids that lived nearby."

Flax rolled his shoulders and winced like his back was aching. "I don't live nearby," he said. "I live about as far away as you can get from here. In Titania."

Amy wrinkled her brow. "What does that mean? If you live so far away, how did you get here?"

"You really do have a lot of questions, don't you?" Flax pushed off the wall and walked toward the left side of the barn. Amy followed him until he came to an oddly positioned door that she hadn't noticed before. It was a sturdy door made of the same aged wood as the rest of the barn, but it was arched, like the entrance to a castle. All around the frame were strange carvings that looked like letters, but Amy couldn't read them.

"I came through there."

Amy looked at the doorway, then looked at Flax, waiting for the punchline of the joke. "What do you mean you came through there? That just leads to the outside of the barn."

"It's a fairy door," Flax said, looking her in the eye. "I came through it because I'm a fairy."

CHAPTER FIVE

Amy narrowed her eyes at him and crossed her arms. What was he trying to pull? "You are not a fairy."

Flax lifted his chin defiantly. "Yes, I am!"

Amy saw something flutter behind his shoulder. A moth? It seemed too big. She cast the beam from her flashlight behind him and was surprised to see the shiny, delicate membranes of wings. They weren't feathery wings like a bird or leathery ones like a bat. These were clear, like glass windowpanes, and they glistened like ice as the light caught them.

Flax obligingly turned so that she could get a better view, and Amy noticed that the top of his left wing was bent unnaturally partway down and the clear delicate membrane was torn.

"Can you see whether it's broken?" he asked, making a pained face.

"You have wings!" Amy gasped.

"Like I said, I'm a fairy. It didn't used to be so hard to convince people, or so I've heard."

"I thought fairies were girls."

"Well, are all humans boys?" he countered mockingly. "Is my wing broken? Can you tell?"

"It looks kinda . . . bent? And part of it is ripped right here . . ."

"Don't touch it!" He jumped back as Amy reached out with her finger. Then he winced when his wing brushed the wall.

"Fine! I was just trying to show you . . ." Amy trailed off. Something was starting to click together in her brain. Earlier today someone had said that only magic could cure her father, and now here she was, face-to-face with a genuine magical fairy—unless this was some sort of trick. But it didn't seem like a trick. Flax seemed genuinely lost and hungry and hurt, and he had wings.

"I have another question. My father is sick; do you have magic that can make him better?"

Flax frowned at her. "What's the matter, don't you humans have doctors anymore?"

"Can you help him or not?"

He sighed. "No, I can't. Listen. Normally, fairies are

obligated to serve humans who save their lives. So I would if I could. But I used up too much magic trying to fix my wing. That iron thing messed it up so much it took most of my magic just to keep me alive. And, on top of that, it takes a lot of power to perform healing magic on a human."

"So . . . you're saying some other fairy might have magic that could cure my father?" she said, pressing on.

Flax rubbed his chin thoughtfully. "That depends. How sick is he? Are we talking about a little head cold or the plague?"

"I don't know exactly. Nobody has told me what he's sick with. But the doctors think he's going to . . . that he won't . . ." She trailed off again and felt her throat tighten up. She turned to face away until she could breathe normally again.

"I see," Flax said, shifting so that he was leaning his good side against the barn wall. "That sounds like a serious illness that would take a lot of magic to cure. The only one who would have enough magic and who also might be willing to help you would be Princess Lily. But . . ."

Amy looked up at him with sudden hope lighting her eyes. She'd been expecting him to say it was impossible, that there wasn't anyone who could help, but there was still a chance! "Great! How do we get to her?" Amy demanded.

Maybe she was dreaming after all and she would wake up in disappointment at any moment. But if there was even the slightest chance that this was all real, that she'd just saved a genuine fairy in her grandmother's old barn and she could ask a fairy princess to cure her father, then she had to take that chance.

"We can't get there. It's impossible," Flax answered, grimly. He scuffed his foot in the dust and folded his arms, scowling into the shadows.

"What do you mean?"

"I told you, I'm out of magic."

"But we just have to go through the door, right?" She pointed at the wooden doorway in the wall, the one he'd called a fairy door. A small wooden handle was fastened into the left side, so the door could be pulled open from inside the barn. As she looked, she thought she could see a glimmer of light shine through the cracks.

"The door is locked and it takes a lot of magic to open it," Flax answered. She could practically hear him rolling his eyes. "And, anyway, you're a human. Even if I had magic enough to get myself through, I'd never be able to bring you."

"I'll try opening it," Amy announced. Something about the fairy door felt familiar, comfortable. Like it was welcoming her. "If I can open it for you, will you help me?"

"Listen, human girl," Flax said with a laugh, "if you can open that door for me, I'll personally escort you all the way to Princess Lily. But there's no way . . ."

Amy reached out, grabbed the wooden handle, and gave it a light tug. The door swung open easily, and a gust of sweet air blew into the barn through the opening.

A shimmering curtain of transparent golden light hung like a veil in the doorway. Through it, Amy could see a sleepy forest glade lit by moonlight.

Smells like a meadow filled with all the fragrant wildflowers in the world wafted through. She breathed it in.

"I think I opened it," she said, turning to look at Flax.

The fairy boy was staring between her and the door with his mouth hanging open. "How did you do that? I've been stuck here trying to open that door for two days!"

"It just opened." She shrugged.

Then she turned to look through the magical doorway, hesitating. If she went through that door, would she ever be able to come back? What if she got stuck on the other side? She thought of her grandmother waking up to find her bed empty and no sign of her anywhere.

Would Amy ever get the chance to see her father again?

Then again, this might be her only chance to find something that would cure him. If she didn't at least try, she would never be able to forgive herself.

She stepped forward, stretching her hand out to touch the golden veil between the worlds. It illuminated her fingers, warming her skin, but she felt no resistance at all.

The doorway seemed to open wider, inviting her to walk through, so she did.

The cool musty air from the barn fell away as the warm fragrance of night blossoms enveloped her. She heard the bubbling, rushing sound of a river nearby.

All around her stood towering trees with enormous trunks covered in moss as thick as cushions and sprinkled with dew that sparkled in the dim blue light that seemed to be coming from everywhere around her.

A river bubbled and sloshed as it wove its way through the forest in front of her.

She was standing on a smooth rock at the base of one of the enormous trees. Behind her, a ponderous root angled up to meet the trunk. Flax appeared, walking out of the dark hollow between the root and tree. He eyed her suspiciously as he stepped out into the light.

"Okay," Amy said, taking a deep breath and looking around with wide eyes. "Did I shrink? Am I fairy-sized now or something? Because these trees look really big."

"Fairy-sized? What's that supposed to mean? Do I look tiny to you?"

"Well, no."

He shook his head but smiled and chuckled incredulously. "No, you didn't shrink. You're just used to small trees."

"But in all the stories I've heard, fairies are tiny," she objected.

"Then you haven't heard the right stories. It is true that some of us learn to make ourselves little. It can be useful for hiding and sneaking into small spaces, but that's really all the good it does."

"So, I'm really in fairyland . . ."

"It does seem so. Incredibly."

"And you're going to take me to the princess so I can ask her for help?"

Flax sighed and rubbed his face with his hands. In the blue glow, Amy could see that, not only was he dirty from hiding out in the barn for two days, he was also barefoot.

"I don't know how I got myself into this, but, yeah. I have to help you. I believe the terms of our contract state that, since you opened the fairy door for me, I have to personally escort you to Princess Lily. And because you gave me an apple, I'm bound to answer all your questions." He made a face. "I'm very disappointed in myself right now, actually."

Amy grinned. "Does that mean that you're like my personal servant?"

Flax scowled. "Don't say that."

Amy raised her eyebrows and kept grinning. "I asked a question. Don't you have to answer all my questions?"

"Ugh, yes, I have to answer your questions. And it does . . . kind of . . . make me your personal servant, in a way."

Amy giggled. "All right then, servant. Take me to your princess!"

Flax rolled his eyes and sighed. "We need to figure out where she is, first."

"Won't she be in her castle or with the king and queen?"

"Probably not. We don't have a king, for one. And she doesn't get along with her sister, the queen. Last I heard, Princess Lily was on the other side of Mt. Oberon, organizing supply lines through the royal city. But that was a few days ago; she could have gone anywhere by now. We need to visit my home first. My mother will probably know where she is."

"Oh." Amy's brow furrowed. She hadn't considered

that finding the princess would be a difficult task at all. She'd thought that once they got through the door, Flax would somehow take her directly to the princess, and she'd be back home within an hour at most.

Flax hopped down to the gravel bank by the river. He winced in pain as he landed, tried to stretch out his wings, and winced again.

Amy hopped down to follow him closely, afraid of being left alone in this strange place.

"So, how are we going to get to your house? Are we going to walk there?"

Flax started walking along the bank while Amy followed him.

"If I had enough magic, or if I could fly, it wouldn't be a problem. But since I'm basically as useless as a human right now"—he turned to raise an eyebrow at her—"we'll have to settle for this." He reached out and pulled aside a heavy curtain of greenery to reveal a small wooden raft hidden in a hollow under the bank.

"As useless as a human, huh? Where would you be if I hadn't come along and saved you?"

He shrugged. "I was hoping one of my friends would figure out where I was and come rescue me. I also thought that if I was healed enough, I might fly to a different door. But . . . after seeing the stars in your world tonight, I knew that was hopeless. Did you know this door comes out completely on the other side of your world from all the others?"

Amy shook her head and shrugged. "I didn't even know there were doors between our worlds. I didn't know fairies or magic existed at all."

Flax eyed her curiously, then shrugged. He walked around behind the raft and started heaving against it, pushing it through the sticky mud and out into the open water.

"Could you help a little?" he asked, panting while Amy stared at him.

"Oh! Right. Yeah." She walked over and started pushing with him. After a few moments of heaving and sloshing, they slid the raft out so that only one corner remained stuck in the mud. The rest of it was floating freely in the shallow river water.

"Go ahead and climb on," Flax told her, wiping sweat from his brow and eyeing the shoreline like he was looking for something.

Amy scrambled aboard on her hands and knees. The raft pitched and water sloshed up over the logs, soaking the lower part of her nightgown.

Flax found what he'd been looking for—a long wooden pole. Carrying it in one hand, he lightly stepped aboard next to Amy, pushing off of the bank with the pole and guiding the raft out into open water.

"It shouldn't be too long before we get down to Lake Village," he told her. "But when we do, you'll need to stay close to me and try not to be noticed, got it?"

"Why?" Amy asked, bracing herself on her hands and knees while the raft pitched some more in the current.

"Like I said before, you're human. You aren't actually supposed to be here. Everyone will notice you if you aren't careful, and word will get around that a human made it into Titania. Then Queen Orchid will find out that I have a secret door to your world she doesn't know about." Flax braced the pole in the riverbed and shoved hard, turning the raft about in a maneuver that made Amy feel dizzy.

"Queen Orchid?" She gasped.

"Princess Lily's sister. If she catches us, this is all over. You'll be lucky if she sends you back to your own world before destroying the door, and even luckier if she sends you to the right place in your world."

"But . . . why would she destroy the door?" Amy asked as they bounced over a rough patch in the current. She was watching Flax in amazement as he stood with effortless balance on the corner of the wobbling raft. "Is she afraid humans will come here and steal your magic?"

Flax shook his head. "No, we aren't afraid of humans. Not here anyway. Here we're safe. But in your own world, you humans have weapons we can't stand against."

"Really? What weapons could be strong enough to fight magic? Bombs?"

He rolled his eyes. "It wasn't a bomb that trashed my wing. It was iron. Iron is lethal to fairies. Even metals with iron in them, like harmless tools and jewelry that you humans wear so casually. We can't bear to touch it."

Amy remembered her own metal sensitivity and felt a twinge of sympathy for Flax.

"Even if it is dangerous in your world, it's still madness to destroy the doors," Flax continued in a quiet voice. "She knows we need rowan berries to make elixir. And no matter what she says, we aren't able to figure out how to grow rowan trees here. They won't even sprout. So we have to use the doors she hasn't destroyed yet to collect the berries, but those are getting fewer and further between. I'm pretty sure that I'm the only one who knows about the door we came through, and it's important that Queen Orchid doesn't find out about it. That means you need to stay hidden."

Amy nodded in understanding. "Got it. If I get caught by the queen, she'll send me back and destroy the door. I'll be careful."

CHAPTER SIX

After a while, the river calmed and ran smoothly down the valley between wooded hills. Flax guided the raft with his pole so they avoided rocks and didn't end up stuck on the bank during sharp turns.

They drifted through a bend in the river, the trees parted, and Amy saw the pale grey expanse of a lake in front of them. She sat up on her knees to get a better view, but Flax put his hand on her shoulder in warning. The current picked up and the inlet pushed them swiftly out into the open water of the lake.

The sudden motion knocked Amy to her side, soaking her nightgown in chilly water even more than it already was.

Standing behind her, still guiding the raft forward, Flax chuckled.

Amy wrung out a section of her cotton nightgown and pulled off her boots to dump the water out. "If you fairies can fly, why would you even bother building a boat?"

He shrugged, still smiling at her in amusement. "Why not? Humans ride horses even if they can walk, don't they? Flying takes energy, and it's nice to rest sometimes. Drifting over the water without the hum of wings in your ears can be pleasant. Look, there's the village!"

Flax pointed ahead to their right. Amy looked and saw what at first seemed to be a handful of small buildings with thatched roofs surrounded by enormous trees shining with Christmas lights.

Then, as she watched, she realized that the lights in the trees were actually coming from windows and streaming through open doorways. Little glittering lights danced like fireflies inside lanterns. Amy wondered if they actually were especially bright fireflies lending their natural light to the fairies.

Flax pushed their raft along the docks at the shoreline, lined with canoes and more glowing lanterns, until they came to the end where the water grew shallow and met the shore with gentle rippling waves.

The soft blue glow from the sky seemed to be growing dimmer as night progressed, and Amy hoped that no one would notice a strange human girl wandering through their village.

Flax hopped off the raft and started pushing it up onto the bank so it wouldn't drift away.

"Well, I'm already soaked," Amy grumbled under her breath as she splashed into the water to help him.

"Thanks." Flax panted, rolling his shoulder and stretching his wings with a grimace.

When they'd beached the raft, Flax grabbed her hand and led her quickly up the waterfront. He pulled her into the dark space between two of the buildings. "Remember what I said about staying hidden," he whispered.

Amy nodded, gazing out at the magical village. Here and there, fairies were flying from house to house on shimmering wings. Flowering vines climbed the trunks of their trees, giving off a rich, sweet scent. The golden glow shining through thousands of windows flickered like candlelight. And, now that she was closer, Amy caught glimpses of the homes within the trees—dark wooden walls here, a corner of a tapestry there, and even a mother rocking her baby while pacing back and forth.

Flax held tightly to Amy's hand while he gazed out into the village. Two fairies passed them, walking along the path—a man and a woman talking quietly together about a butternut harvest.

Flax motioned for Amy to wait and be quiet. She held her breath.

The two fairies moved on, not noticing them.

Flax squeezed Amy's hand and hurried forward. She followed as quickly as she could. Water sloshed in her boots, and her wet nightgown clung to her skin. Even though the night was warm, she started shivering—or maybe she was just trembling with nerves.

They rushed around the corner of another building and paused again. Flax looked all around and overhead, then pulled Amy along into an open archway at the base of the nearest giant tree.

"Phew!" Flax panted, releasing her hand. "I wasn't sure we'd be able to do that."

Amy was breathing heavily, too.

She was still trembling all over, but now she was too preoccupied admiring the inside of the fairy house to worry about being cold.

"This is your home?"

"Yeah, it's been in my family for generations." Flax grabbed a handful of nuts out of a wooden bowl and started munching on them.

It was hard to believe that any tree could be big enough to hold an entire house inside of it, but the living room was a comfortable size, with wooden chairs, cabinets, hanging lanterns, and even a bookshelf against the wall next to the window. Amy marveled at the intricate vine and flower designs etched into the woodwork.

"Flax? Flax! Why were you gone so long? I knew you should have told me where that door was. And who is—"

Amy whirled around to see who was speaking.

It was a fairy woman, and her voice cut off suddenly when she got a look at Amy.

She was short and full-figured, with raven-black hair pulled into an elegant knot at the back of her head. She stood in a way that made Amy think she was an authority figure not to be crossed. Her lips parted in amazement and her dark eyes widened in wonder as she gazed at Amy.

For a moment, Amy was simply struck by the beauty of this fairy. She thought that she must be meeting somebody important. She wanted to make a good first impression, so she did her best to curtsy, but she'd never learned how and it felt a little awkward.

Flax cleared his throat and smiled. Amy got the impression that he was trying not to laugh.

"Mother, I would like you to meet Miss Amy," Flax announced. "Amy, this is my mother, Marigold."

His mother? Amy gaped in awe. Marigold had her

wings folded over her back, but they fluttered slightly, like she was fidgeting nervously. She looked between Amy and Flax for a moment. "Flax . . . how . . . why . . . what are you *thinking*, bringing her here?"

Flax grimaced and looked down at his feet. "I'm sorry, Mother. It was an accident and a foolish mistake."

Marigold waited, her eyes darting between the two of them and occasionally to the window.

"I was wounded and trapped in the human world. This girl helped me, and I made an agreement to take her to Princess Lily."

His mother's eyes hardened. "You had no business agreeing to something like that. Couldn't you have offered a wish or a charmed trinket if you needed her help? And how did you manage to bring her through the door?"

He shrugged and winced as the motion jostled his wing. "I can't grant her wish. I'm not powerful enough. And I didn't think she'd be able to open the door, so I thought she'd renege on her end and I wouldn't be bound. I was being sarcastic, but then she did it. She opened the door by herself. If it hadn't been for Amy, I'd still be trapped there."

Marigold looked at Amy curiously.

Amy waved shyly. She hadn't really understood everything Flax said.

Her nightgown was dripping on the smooth wooden floor, creating a small puddle under her, but Flax's mother didn't seem to mind.

Then the fairy turned her eyes back to Flax. "What happened to your wing? Let me see."

Flax turned around. His mother took the lantern from the windowsill and brought it close to examine his damaged wing. Flax grimaced as she grasped it gingerly and stretched it out. "That was a close one. It looks like you nearly snapped your left forewing. It's bent here right at the nodus. Come to the kitchen and I'll make you a splint."

She held the lantern high and looked at Amy. "You come, too, human child. We have some talking to do."

Marigold turned and strode through an arched passage to the kitchen. Flax gave Amy a look that said *we'd better do what she says* and followed after her. Amy meekly trailed behind.

The fairy's kitchen was not like anything Amy had seen inside a house before. The walls were covered with hanging dried herbs, bottles of liquid, shelves filled with clay jars, baskets, and bottles, and bundles of grain. The floor was filled with boxes containing mysterious ingredients and barrels bound in rope. All along the right wall, large, round windows let in the soft blue light and sleepy scent of flowers from outside. Another large archway led to an outer courtyard where a dark clay pot hung suspended over glowing red coals.

Flax sat on a little wooden stool in the middle of the room, and his mother rummaged in a basket until she found a thick reed and strips of white cloth. She took the items to Flax, braced his wing with the reed and began carefully wrapping the strips of cloth around it to hold it in place.

"So, little girl," she said as she worked, "tell me how you got here."

Amy jumped when the fairy addressed her, and she wrung her hands together. "It's just like he said. I opened the door and came through. Flax said that the princess has enough magic to cure my father, so I want to find her and ask for her help."

"You're looking for healing magic?"

"For my father, yes. He's very ill. The doctors think he won't . . . he won't live much longer."

Marigold tucked in the last bit of cloth and made a gesture over it with her hand. The cloth seemed to tighten and smooth out, fitting perfectly over Flax's wing.

"If he is that ill, it would take powerful magic to save him," Marigold agreed, nodding.

A fussy whimper came from the darkened room on the other side of the kitchen. Marigold stood and hurried out. She returned a moment later with a little fairy baby so chubby and wiggly that Amy couldn't help but step closer for a better look.

"Did you bring the rowan berries?" Marigold asked Flax, bouncing the baby in her arms. "I've been trying to soothe him with milkweed, but it isn't helping much anymore."

"Yes! Yes, I have some right here." Flax tugged on the cords of his pouch, opening it, and poured the little orange berries into a wooden bowl on the counter.

"Oh, thank heavens! Here, take your brother." Marigold handed the baby off to Flax, and he grunted under the weight. Amy could see that Flax's little brother had small blue wings that looked much too small to fly with yet.

Marigold selected a single orange rowan berry and dropped it into a small stone bowl on the table. Then she took a stone pestle and began rhythmically crushing the berry into a paste.

“It'll be all right, Acorn,” Flax murmured to the baby fairy. “You'll get your elixir soon. Mother is making some right now.”

Amy noticed that baby Acorn was more pale than his big brother. His skin had a grayish tinge to it. Was he sick?

Marigold added a few drops of fluid from a little

blue bottle to the stone bowl. Then she took a clay teapot from a ledge near the exit and poured hot water over the mixture. The paste thickened and started glowing purple.

She carefully poured the contents of the bowl into a clay container of water about the size of a milk jug. As the thick paste oozed into the water, it blended together. Soon the whole thing was filled with a glowing purple mixture as thick as maple syrup and smelled—Amy stepped closer and sniffed—like blueberry muffins.

CHAPTER SEVEN

Little Acorn continued to fuss while his mother worked, and then he finally started crying loudly. Flax bounced him in his arms and rocked him, making gentle, soothing noises.

Marigold poured some of the syrupy purple mixture into a small wooden cup shaped like a flower bud. The top half of the cup snapped into place leaving a little opening at the tip of the flower bud. When it was ready, she gently took Acorn into her arms and offered it to him.

Amy watched as the baby fairy put the cup to his lips and began drinking the juice greedily. His color slowly began to improve. His skin started to look healthier. His whimpers died down, and he sighed in contentment.

"Is . . . is he sick? What's wrong?" Amy asked.

Marigold shook her head as she laid the baby in a bassinet by the wall. “No, not sick. He just needed some elixir.” She returned to the jug and poured a little of the elixir into two more cups. She handed one of them to Flax, and he drank it immediately. Marigold drank the other cup herself, and Amy noticed that she stood taller and a flush of rainbow colors spread through her wings that hadn’t been there before.

“Flax said that fairies need rowan berries to live . . .”

Marigold pulled a large basket out of a cabinet in the wall. When she opened it, Amy saw dozens of small glass vials. Flax immediately got up, grabbed the jug, and started helping his mother fill the vials with the glowing purple elixir.

“We’re more similar to humans than you might think,” she said, squeezing a little cork into one of the vials. “In your world, for example, people need to eat salt. If you don't, you become very ill and can die. This has been a problem for humans in the past, when salt has been scarce.”

"Really?"

Marigold nodded. “I remember when men used to work long hours and get paid in salt instead of money, and they were glad to do it. For our kind, there is a different scarcity. Fairies need the fruit of the rowan tree to make elixir or our magic dies. If our magic dies, we die. But we can't get rowan trees to grow here in Titania, so we have to visit the human world to collect the berries."

"It's getting more difficult, though," Flax said, pouring the last of the elixir into one of the vials. "Queen Orchid has already destroyed most of the doors to your world. She thinks if we can't get the berries there, we'll finally figure out a way to grow rowan trees here. But it's madness! If we could grow them here, we already would have."

"Hush!" his mother scolded. "Don't speak ill of the queen. Remember where you are." She nodded to the open archway that led outside.

Flax blushed and nodded repentantly. "It's true, though," he muttered.

"It is dangerous in the human world," Marigold continued, as though to change the subject. "Iron, when it is collected and fashioned into tools and weapons . . . we can't stand against it. And there is so much iron in the human world these days it's nearly impossible to avoid it."

"Yeah, look what happened to me," Flax said, wiggling his injured wing in Amy's direction. It didn't seem to be hurting him so much anymore.

"You were hurt by iron?" His mother gasped in

alarm, turning away from sorting the vials on a shelf to stare at him.

In his bassinet, baby Acorn wiggled and fussed in his sleep.

Flax grimaced and shrugged. "Yeah . . . I fell on some kind of farm tool."

Marigold walked across the room to look at his back again, more closely this time. "I'm surprised it wasn't worse. Oh, Flax, you could have—"

"That's how I got stuck there," he explained while his mother kept looking between his wing and his face in concern. "I used too much magic healing myself. If I hadn't healed, I wouldn't have made it. But then I was too weak to make it back through the door."

"And this girl helped you . . ."

He nodded. "Yes, she fed me, and somehow she opened the door, too."

Marigold took a deep breath and nodded solemnly, seeming to finally wrap her mind around what had happened. She faced Amy with glistening eyes. "Then you have saved my son's life, and I will stand by his vow as well."

"Mother?"

She waved her hand at him dismissively. "You can't break your vow anyway. And by saving you, she's saved our whole family and many others as well. We *all* owe her." She turned back to Amy. "You want an audience with Princess Lily, is that it?"

Amy nodded. "I want her to heal my father." Amy paused, thinking. "And I need to get back home before my grandmother wakes up in the morning . . . by sunrise."

Marigold pursed her lips, eyeing Amy appraisingly. "Hmm, then the first thing we ought to do is get you out of those wet clothes and into a disguise. The disguise won't fool anyone for long if they see you up close, but at a glance, it should work."

Flax's mother guided Amy through the house to her boudoir. This was another fascinating room that looked very different from what Amy would have expected. There was a bed with a light-green silk curtain draped around it. Round, open windows lined the wall, letting in the dim glow and gentle breeze from outside. Red and green cushions with intricate embroidered designs sat in piles around the room. The floor was covered in a rich-brown woven carpet. Amy had removed her water-logged boots in the kitchen, and the carpet felt delightfully soft under her bare feet.

Marigold kneeled in front of a large wooden trunk, rummaged around in it for a moment, and pulled out a few different dresses, each more gorgeous than the last.

She examined each gown in turn and shook her head, tossing them aside one by one.

Finally, she pulled out a gown of deep forest green with a black ivy design embroidered around the hem. Among the dark embroidery, tiny glints of light flashed, like the fabric was woven with diamonds.

"Ah, this should do," Marigold said, standing up and holding the dress out at arm's length with a smile. "You'll look just like a forest fairy from a distance."

Amy bit her lip nervously and stepped closer. The dress was so beautiful she was afraid to put it on. Surely she would ruin it somehow.

"Are you sure it will fit me?"

"This was one of my dresses when I was about your size. The fabric stretches and moves as you do. I'm sure it will be very comfortable. Try it on."

Marigold left her for a minute so Amy could pull her wet nightgown off and slip the dress over her head. The fabric was remarkably soft. It smelled like cedar and felt even more comfortable than her favorite pajamas. She twirled once, watching the dress flare out gracefully, the tiny invisible jewels sparkling around her in the lantern light.

"It's so beautiful," she said, grinning broadly at Marigold when she returned.

"It looks lovely on you." The fairy smiled. "And now

for the hair," she announced, brandishing a comb and a bowl of white flowers and ribbons.

Amy sat on a pile of cushions while Marigold began combing and weaving her hair into braids. Amy felt the tightening of her hair and slight prickle as flower stems twisted against her scalp.

"I often wondered what it would be like to have daughters," Marigold murmured. "My mother used to do this for me, but I can barely get Flax to let me cut his hair to keep it out of his eyes."

Marigold laughed and Amy giggled with her.

"What about my hair?" Flax poked his head into the room, frowning suspiciously.

"Oh, nothing, dear," his mom answered, smiling. She made one last twist and tied two small braids together at the back of Amy's head. "There we are. What do you think?"

Amy looked up at Flax to see his reaction.

He was staring at her with wide eyes. "Wow! How did you do that, Mother? She almost looks like a fairy."

"It wasn't anything I did. I just dressed her for the part. She has the right features already." Flax's mother raised Amy's chin with her fingertips to examine her face thoughtfully.

There were no mirrors in the fairy house, so Amy had to be content with the reactions of Flax and

Marigold, and they assured her she looked enough like a fairy to pass as one at a glance. Marigold even gave her a black traveling cloak to wear over her dress which would help disguise the fact that she had no wings. When Amy draped it over her shoulders, Flax smiled and nodded in approval.

"You really do almost look like a fairy," he assured her. "I'm amazed."

"All right, now for the difficult part," his mother said. "You need to get to the princess and back home before sunrise, right?"

"Yeah, that's right. I don't want my grandmother to wake up and notice that I'm gone."

"I can't go with you, because I'm needed here in the village, but I do have word of where the princess might be." She looked at Flax.

"Is it far?" he asked.

Marigold lowered her voice. "She moved forces in to protect the gate in the Crystal Cavern. Rumor is, that is the queen's next target, so the Guardians are focusing on defending that gate. The princess should be with them."

"The Guardians?"

"Fairies who are working against the queen," Flax whispered. "She calls us 'rebels,' but we're just trying to keep her from destroying all the doors."

"Oh, I see," Amy whispered back. "I guess the queen won't appreciate that very much."

Marigold shook her head sadly. "No, she doesn't. Her prison is full of fairies who found that out the hard way."

Flax frowned and looked away.

"So we need to get to the Crystal Cavern to find the Guardians and that's where the princess will be?" Amy asked.

"I believe that's your best chance, and I trust that Flax can get you there; he knows the way." She turned to her son. "How is your wing feeling now?"

Flax took a deep breath, shaking out of his sudden melancholy, and stretched his wings out behind him. It didn't seem to hurt, so he fluttered them once and smiled. "It's already feeling much better. The elixir helped a lot."

"It will still take time before your magic is restored, don't forget. Only use your magic in emergencies until you've fully recovered."

"Of course, Mother. Don't worry, I'll remember."

Marigold led the two of them back out to the kitchen where Flax started filling his pouch with vials of elixir.

Amy was about to ask him what he was doing when Marigold drew her aside.

"I want you to drink this," she said, offering Amy one of the vials.

"Your magic elixir? But . . ."

"Something tells me that it might help you," Marigold said. "In any case, it won't hurt. It's a very nutritious blend for humans and will give you plenty of energy."

"Will it give me magic?" She looked over at Flax, who was watching them curiously. "And . . . don't you need it?"

Marigold smiled. "The elixir only restores magic to magical creatures. It won't give magic to an ordinary human. If it wasn't for you, we wouldn't have the rowan berries to make it and my son would still be stuck in your world with no hope of returning. So I want you to drink it."

Amy took the vial in her hand, pulled out the cork, and sniffed the fluid.

"It smells different to everyone," Flax said. "To fairies, it usually smells like our favorite food."

"It reminds me of blueberry muffins," Amy told him with a shrug. "I don't think it's my favorite food, but I like it."

She felt a little nervous with Flax and Marigold staring at her. She hesitated, wondering why they were watching her so closely, like they were expecting something to happen. Then she brought the vial to her lips and drank.

The elixir felt warm and thick in her mouth. It tasted sweet, like blueberries and butter and cream. It tingled in her throat and warmed her belly. The warmth grew and radiated out, banishing the chill from being soaked in the river and filling her with energy. She felt alert and awake, ready to face anything.

"How do you feel?" Flax asked. He sounded casual, but he was still staring at her intensely.

"I feel fine. It's very good. Only I'm not sure you should have wasted it on me. I don't need to drink that stuff to live like you do."

Flax pursed his lips.

Marigold smiled at her and took the empty vial, but Amy thought she looked a little disappointed. Maybe they'd been expecting something special to happen.

"It's the least we could do," she said. "Now hurry, you two. The sooner you get to the Crystal Cavern, the easier it will be to find the princess and send Amy home."

Flax ran his fingers through his dark hair and grinned at Amy. "Don't worry. The cavern isn't too far away."

He took her hand and led her outside into the night.

CHAPTER EIGHT

Flax seemed less cautious than he had been before as he guided her along the nearly empty walkway through Lake Village. The shining lanterns and warm glow from windows gave light enough for everyone to see outside. Amy was in awe, feeling like she was walking through a galaxy of stars.

"Just act natural," Flax murmured as they passed a trio of fairy girls walking together.

"Hello, Flax!" a green-haired fairy called as they passed. "Who's your new friend?"

"Just a pixie I met while rafting today," Flax answered, smiling nervously.

All three girls turned to look at Amy.

"My mother has more elixir now!" Flax blurted hastily.

"She does?" one of the girls asked.

"Freshly made tonight!"

The girls jumped into the air and flew away in a whirl of humming wings and wind.

"Phew, that was close." Flax sighed, continuing down the road with Amy following.

"Just act natural," Amy reminded him primly.

Flax chuckled. "Right. I guess I forgot that part. Come on, let's get out of the village before someone else notices you."

He guided her the rest of the way through Lake Village, positioning himself between Amy and any passersby, trying to keep her as inconspicuous as possible.

The road led uphill away from the lake, through a valley, and between two dark hills that towered ahead of them.

Once they had left the village, Flax took them off the road and they started climbing one of the hills. The incline was steep and the ground soft. Amy's feet sank into the grass and moss. It felt like she was climbing a tower of pillows. Soon, she was panting in her effort to keep up with Flax.

"Don't you have cars or horses or anything?" She gasped, scrambling over a mossy boulder.

"Well, this is usually a lot easier with wings," Flax said, but he wasn't even out of breath from the climb.

Amy screwed up her face and trudged ahead. The warmth of the rowan juice elixir still tingled in her arms and legs. She wondered if it was giving her enough energy to climb the hill. If she hadn't taken it, would she have collapsed from exhaustion by now?

The hill leveled off after a while, descending into a little gully filled with fragrant blossoming trees and bushes. Fireflies danced in the shadows.

"There's an entrance to the caverns here," Flax said. "One of the rivers that feeds our lake runs under the mountains and through these hills, and that's what formed the caverns. This entrance isn't well known, so don't tell anyone about it."

"Okay." She shrugged. As if she would ever have the opportunity or desire to tell anyone about a secret entrance to an underground cavern in fairyland.

Flax led her down into the gully. The ground hardened, making it easier to walk, and soon Amy was picking her way over large stones and thick roots. Clouds of fireflies scattered as they approached. Moonlight glinted off the delicate strands of spider webs that were stretched between bushes and tree branches.

Together, they approached a cliff face in the mountain, and Flax showed her a crack in the wall hidden behind a giant boulder. It was completely dark inside.

"Can fairies see in the dark?" Amy asked, nervously. "I can't see anything in there."

"I can't see in there either, but don't worry. Just follow me; it will get better."

Flax crept into the hole, and Amy could only follow, feeling the cool stone walls and listening to the soft sounds of his movement in front of her.

After a few paces, the roof of the passageway sloped downward, and Amy and Flax were forced to crawl ahead on their hands and knees. The darkness was so complete that Amy could almost feel it pressing against her on all sides. She could hear the echoes of their breathing bouncing off the walls and ceiling of the tunnel.

The passage narrowed even further, and she could hear Flax scooting ahead on his belly, with barely enough room for his wings to fit without scraping the stone roof.

Amy felt a surge of panic. She'd never liked feeling trapped. Being in a room with a closed door and no window was enough to make her nervous. Here, in the absolute darkness with hard rock walls all around her, the only thing keeping her moving was the thought that she was moving toward something that would save her father.

But this? Squeezing into a hole in the ground like a worm?

She stopped, trembling and whimpering in fear.

She heard Flax scraping and scrabbling over the dirt through the tunnel in front of her. "It's okay, Amy," he called. "Just come through. It opens up."

Still trembling, Amy lowered herself to her belly and started slinking through the narrow tunnel. It was horrible! She could feel the walls pressing against her sides and sensed the weight of the mountain, thousands of tons of rock and earth, pressing down around her. The cool, dank, still air made her feel like she was trapped in a grave. The darkness before her eyes, though unchanged, felt closer to her face, wrapping around her body as she wiggled forward. And worst of all, her movements were restricted by the dead-cold rock all around her, pressing into her belly, keeping her from lifting her head or stretching out her arms. She could barely inch forward with the limited movement the space allowed.

Then something clasped onto her hand and started tugging.

Amy screamed.

"Hey! It's just me! I'm helping you get out." Flax's voice came from above her head.

"Oh." Amy felt her face get hot with embarrassment. Fortunately, it was too dark for Flax to notice.

She gave him her other hand, too, and he pulled hard, sliding her out of the little tunnel.

Once she was out, Amy sat with her back against the wall, panting.

"That part was the worst," Flax confessed. "Being confined like that is torture to fairies, but I've done this enough that I know how to go through quickly. That makes it more bearable."

"I don't like to feel trapped either." Amy shuddered. "It's horrible, especially when I feel like I can't move."

Flax took her hand again and helped her up. Amy stood cautiously, afraid that she might knock her head against the ceiling, but there was plenty of room in this new space.

Flax led her forward, still holding on to Amy's hand. The air grew cooler, and the echoes of their footsteps sounded far away. It felt like a much bigger place than the other tunnels they'd been in so far.

They walked close to the wall, Flax feeling his way along the stone with his free hand. Then they turned a corner and Amy caught a glimpse of a faint blue light ahead. The light shone through a tall branching crack in the wall, looking almost like a glowing blue tree.

Flax led her toward it, and Amy realized that the crevice in the wall was even bigger than she'd thought at first. As they approached, the opening appeared to grow bigger and bigger until she could see walls inside the stone passage at the base. When they reached it, there was more than enough room for Amy and Flax to walk through side by side.

The glow wasn't coming from the other side of the wall, Amy realized. The walls themselves were coated in a thin layer of some soft glowing substance. She brushed her finger against it; the glow brightened slightly at her touch, but her skin came away clean.

"What is this stuff?" she asked.

"We call it glow moss," Flax murmured. "It's really a kind of lichen. It wouldn't normally grow down here, but we brought it in to help light up the caverns." Flax stopped and opened up his pouch, pulling out a short stone blade. "Watch this."

He scraped the blade against the wall, and the glow moss came up, sticking to itself and forming a clump. Flax scraped some more until he had a fist-sized clump of the bright glowing substance.

He put his blade back into his pouch and collected the glow moss in his hands.

Amy watched as he pressed it together, squeezing it into a ball. The glow moss brightened with every squeeze of his hands until it was almost too bright to look at.

"Pretty neat, right?" he said, grinning in the blue-white light.

"Yeah, that is pretty cool."

They continued forward. The passage they were walking through curved around to the left. As they made the turn, Amy noticed an old male fairy sitting on the ground with his back braced against the wall in front of where the passage opened up again.

When he saw them, he jumped up alertly, his white beard and hair wild, his eyes flashing. He pointed his crystal-tipped spear at them, threateningly. Then he paused, blinking at Flax with recognition. "Flax? Is that you?"

"Of course it's me, Bromeliad," Flax scoffed. "Who put you on guard duty? Haven't you fallen asleep one too many times for that?"

Bromeliad narrowed his eyes and grunted. "Too many of the Guardians are falling ill. We need everyone we can get. And where have you been? Running around with some pixie?" He thrust his spear toward Amy accusingly.

"She's a friend," Flax said firmly, stepping in front of

Amy to block Bromeliad's view. "I need to take her to see Princess Lily. Is she in the cavern?"

Bromeliad looked back at Flax and scoffed. "And what claim does this pixie have to see the princess? I'll let *you* in, of course, but her? How do I know we can trust her? She could be a spy for the queen."

"She isn't a spy." Flax put his hands on his hips, rolling his eyes. "Isn't my word worth trusting anymore?"

"Of course I'm not a spy!" Amy pushed her way around Flax to stare fiercely at the old fairy.

Flax tried to stop her, but she was angry. "Why would Flax bring a spy in?" she demanded. "I've only known him for a couple hours and I can already tell he'd never betray the princess."

Bromeliad was staring at her with his eyes widened in shock. "A human!" He glared at Flax. "You brought a human child into Titania? Into the Crystal Cavern?" His eyes narrowed suspiciously. "She came through that secret door of yours, didn't she? How did you get her through? You have to put her back where you found her!"

Amy quailed with guilt, stepping back behind Flax. She should have let him take care of things. She was supposed to be staying hidden! What was she thinking?

"I can't take her back yet, Bromeliad," Flax explained. "I have an onus to abate first."

"You made a deal with a *human?*" Bromeliad was starting to look pale. The spear trembled in his hands.

"I'm afraid so . . ."

Flax started to explain to the older fairy what had happened and why Amy needed to see the princess. While they were talking, Amy peered through the opening at the end of the passage, trying to see into the next cavern.

Through the opening, she could hear the gentle murmurs of other fairies talking together. Then a group of them started to sing. It was a beautiful and sad song that made her want to smile and cry at the same time.

Unconsciously, she stepped around Flax and past Bromeliad to try to look into the cavern and see the singers.

"Hey now!" Bromeliad shouted, trying to block her.

Startled, Amy jumped back and pushed him away at the same time. Even though she hadn't pushed very hard, Bromeliad stumbled and crumpled to the ground with a groan.

"Bromeliad! What's wrong?" Flax cried, rushing to the older fairy's side.

"I didn't push him hard!" Amy said. "He surprised me, that's all. Is he okay?"

Flax wasn't paying attention to her. He knelt beside the old fairy, lifting his head and taking his hand. Bromeliad looked very pale compared to Flax; it wasn't just the blue light as Amy had thought. He was sweating and his wings trembled weakly. He was obviously very ill.

CHAPTER NINE

"Foolish imp," Bromeliad gasped, blinking at Flax. "You know what's wrong. The same thing's wrong with everyone these days. We need elixir."

Flax sighed and drew the strings on his pouch. "I thought they always gave an extra ration to the guards." He reached into the pouch and drew out one of the tiny vials of glowing purple elixir. He popped the cork out with his thumb and handed it to Bromeliad.

The old fairy glanced at the vial and back up to Flax, suspiciously. "Where did you get this?" he asked.

"It's a new batch. The human girl isn't the only thing I brought back with me." He chuckled. "I managed to collect some rowan berries, too. I've brought more for our supplies here."

Bromeliad drank the elixir, and Amy could see that

he immediately started to breathe easier. His color returned, and his hands stopped shaking.

"From your secret door, no doubt." Bromeliad smiled knowingly at Flax. "When are you going to tell us all where that is?"

"I won't," Flax said flatly. "If everyone knew where it was, we'd have to post guards there, too. There aren't enough of us to protect the known doors as it is."

Bromeliad pushed himself to his feet and brushed the dust off his knees. "Very sensible of you. You're sounding more like your father every day. But elixir is growing more and more scarce. Having new places for harvesting parties might save some lives."

Flax's face fell, and he ran a hand through his black hair nervously. "I . . . I know, Bromeliad. And I'm bringing in as many as I can. It's just . . ."

Bromeliad patted Flax's shoulder gruffly. "I understand. Go on in. There are others in the cavern who need elixir more than I did. Just be sure to keep that girl out of mischief while you're in there." He gestured to Amy with his spear without even looking at her.

"What mischief?" Amy scoffed.

"Thank you, Bromeliad," Flax said, ignoring her. "I promise I'll keep her out of trouble."

"You'd better," the old fairy rumbled, warily watching Flax and Amy as they walked into the cavern.

Amy turned back to give him a piercing look while he took up an alert guard stance against the wall. He appeared much stronger and more alert than he had when she first saw him—the elixir worked very fast.

Flax took Amy along a narrow descending walkway into the Crystal Cavern.

At first, Amy was dazzled by the amount of light in the open space. Instead of the dim blue bioluminescence of the glow moss, the cavern shone with a bright white light reflected and refracted through sparkling crystals all around them.

As her eyes adjusted to the light, she saw that, while the hard floor beneath them was white granite, the walls and ceiling were entirely made up of clear, shining crystals. If it had been colder, Amy might have thought that she was inside a mountain of ice.

The light refracting through the pillars and columns cast beams in every color of the rainbow; tiny flashes of red, blue, yellow, and violet caught Amy's eye as she looked around.

As they descended the walkway, the open floor of the Crystal Cavern came into view. In the center rested a shallow, oval-shaped pool with what looked like a giant water lily made of white crystal floating in the middle.

More fairies were in the cavern, too. Two were guarding the crystal water lily. Four more were standing near the entrance to another passageway at the ground level. A group of fairies was standing together near the far wall; these were the ones who were still singing the haunting melody that Amy was so drawn to. A few other fairies were seated off to the side, eating colorful fruit from small wooden bowls, and another group was lying down in a little hollow, apparently asleep, surrounded by small crystalline stalagmites.

As they walked, Amy searched through the gathered fairies with her eyes wondering which one might be the princess. All of the female fairies were unbelievably beautiful and dressed stunningly—it could be any one of them. She would be meeting her soon and, with luck, would be headed home with a cure shortly after.

She felt a thrill of excitement and gratitude for Flax. As soon as she got home and healed her father, she vowed that she would collect as many rowan berries as she could and send them through the fairy door for him.

Flax walked her out into the courtyard and around the pool. The guard fairies eyed her curiously, their silver armor gleaming in the white light, but they didn't seem to notice that she was a human; their eyes looked wary but not alarmed.

Amy watched the crystal lily as they passed, wondering what was so special about it. Then she noticed that the door-shaped space between the central petals was dark, which was unusual because nothing else in the cavern was dark. It looked like the entrance to a tunnel, just as the door under the tree to her grandmother's barn had appeared. That crystal lily must be the fairy door.

Flax ignored the guards and led Amy around the pool to the group of fairies who had just finished singing.

Amy stayed behind him, hoping that she wouldn't be noticed.

"Flax, you've returned!" a dark-skinned fairy exclaimed. She wore a shimmering purple dress and had her hair pulled up in a tightly braided bun, studded with green gems. Her wings, which she kept folded against her back, were mostly transparent with a few black patterns that shone iridescently in the light.

"We feared you must have been caught," another fairy said. This one was shorter, with lightly tan skin and short hair so blonde it was almost white. She wore a bright yellow dress, and her fluttering wings shimmered with shades of green.

"Zinnia, Clover." Flax nodded to them in turn. "It's nice to see you, too. I was stuck on the other side for a while, that's all." He shrugged.

"You were trapped?" Clover gasped, putting her hand to her throat in alarm.

Flax tried to shrug it off while he worked the strings of his pouch loose again. "Not trapped, exactly. I just couldn't get the door open for a while. It's no big deal." Flax looked over at the fairies who were lying down. "What's with Cardamom and Juniper? And why were you singing the mourning song?" His eyes opened wide with horror and he looked up at them again. "They're not . . ."

"Not yet," Zinnia assured him. "They're weak, and we don't have enough elixir for everyone. We're expecting the group from Mirror Pool to bring some supplies in soon."

Flax finally got his pouch open and gave a handful of vials to Zinnia. "Make sure these get to the ones who need it most," he told her.

Other fairies started gathering around them as well, looking at the vials with wide eyes.

"You got some berries, then!" one of the male fairies said.

Zinnia handed a few of the vials to others, and they fluttered toward where the ill fairies lay on the floor.

"Of course he did," Clover said, grinning at Flax. "Flax always comes through."

"Who's your little friend?" Zinnia asked, handing the last of the vials to Clover and looking curiously at Amy. "She's not much of a talker, is she?"

The rest of the group of fairies dispersed, passing the vials of elixir out to those who needed it, but Zinnia stayed.

Flax stepped lightly to the side so the fairy could see her. "This . . . is *Amy*," he said, adding a slight emphasis to Amy's human name.

Zinnia's eyes widened and she looked at Flax with a shocked expression.

Amy was shocked, too. He'd been adamant about keeping her a secret, but now he basically just told someone she was human. Maybe he trusted these fairies more than the others they'd met.

"Yes, she's human," he said. "But without her, I wouldn't have made it back this time. And I made a deal with her to take her to Princess Lily."

"You're sure she's really human? How did you bring a human to Titania? Kind of looks like a fairy to me."

"That's because Flax's mother gave me this disguise," Amy said, holding out her skirt. "I'm definitely a human. I don't have wings or anything." She noticed the guard fairies around the crystal lily eyeing her with renewed suspicion. "I'm sorry. I know I don't belong here. This place is probably very special to all of you. I'll go home as soon as I can, but I need to see the princess first."

Zinnia stared at Amy's face for a moment longer with her lips pressed together in concentration. Then she relaxed and shook her head sadly. "I'm afraid the princess isn't here anymore. We got word that the queen is changing her plans and moving on the Titania Door."

Flax gasped. "She wouldn't! The palace door? The door Queen Titania built herself? How could she?"

Zinnia frowned. "She means to destroy them all. None of the doors are safe."

Flax groaned in frustration. "Nobody even uses that door anymore! What purpose would it serve to destroy it?"

Zinnia didn't seem to have a response to this. They stood together in silent despair for a long moment.

"Um . . . so . . . where is the palace?" Amy asked, hesitantly.

"You intend to try to stop her?" Zinnia looked sharply at Amy. "That's impossible. A human child wouldn't stand a chance against the queen of Titania. You cannot begin to comprehend the power of her magic."

"Well, yes. I mean . . . no. I mean, I don't want to try to stop her. That is, I hope someone does, but . . ."

"Amy's thinking of Princess Lily," Flax explained. "We need to find her. If the princess has gone to the palace, that's where we need to go, too." He turned to Amy with a resigned expression. "The palace is on the other side of Mt. Oberon, a long way from here."

"On the other side of the mountain?" Amy asked in alarm. "How long will it take to get there? Will we be able to get there in time for me to go home by morning?"

Flax paused and thought for a moment, furrowing his brow and rubbing his chin in concentration. "It might be possible. I might be able to come up with an idea to get us there with enough time, but we'll have to hurry."

Zinnia suddenly grabbed Flax's arm and turned him to face her. "Listen to me," she said. "Going to the palace is nothing like coming here. In these outer towns, Queen Orchid is not in favor, but at the palace, there are powerful fairies who are loyal to her. If they discover that you brought a human here, how long do you think it will take for them to figure out that you have a secret door? How long do you think it will take them to trace you back to us?"

Amy gulped and Flax nodded solemnly.

Flax was about to say something in response—he was opening his mouth to speak—but then another fairy flew in through the passage from outside. He wore orange clothing and had short red hair. His face was red from exertion, and when he landed, his tan wings continued to flutter in alarm. Most of the fairies in the cavern came to stand around him.

"What's the matter, Cestrum?" one of the fairies asked.

"The Mirror Pool," he gasped. "The queen! She's been to the Mirror Pool. The door is destroyed!"

The gathered fairies gasped and groaned in dismay.

"The Mirror Pool?"

"No!"

"It can't be!"

"We'd heard the queen was in the south!" Zinnia said.

Cestrum shook his head, still breathing heavily and mopping his brow with his sleeve. "She came upon us at the Mirror Pool shortly after Princess Lily left. It was as though she knew we would be undefended there."

"Could she have actually known?" Flax mumbled.

"What's the Mirror Pool?" Amy whispered to him while the other fairies fretted and fluttered around the exhausted messenger, pelting him with questions.

"It's one of the oldest doors in Titania . . ." Flax frowned. "Or it was. It was our most reliable source of rowan berries, too. There are no trees near the other side of this door anymore." He nodded to the crystal water lily behind them. "Now the Mirror Pool door is gone, and that means that the Palace Door and the Crystal Cavern are the last known doors to the human world."

Amy drew him away from the group. “And the princess is the only one who can stop her?”

Flax nodded. “Together, we can slow her down a little, but we aren’t strong enough to protect the gate for long. If only Princess Lily had been there!” He clenched his teeth in anger, but Amy could see tears glistening in his eyes, too.

“Could she have known that the princess wouldn’t be there?” Amy asked.

“I don’t know . . . it’s possible. Maybe?”

“Because, if she knew that the princess wasn’t there, maybe she knows that this door is also unprotected right now.”

Flax’s head snapped up, and he looked at Amy in shocked horror. “You’re right! Cestrum!” He turned back to the group and ran to the exhausted fairy. “Where did Queen Orchid go after leaving the Mirror Pool?”

“I . . . I don’t know. Hey, is that a human child?”

“Don’t worry about that right now!” Flax yelled as other fairies turned to stare at Amy. “Did she fly north after leaving the door?”

Cestrum coughed once and shook his head. “No, she wasn’t heading north. Her entourage flew southwest, I believe.”

Flax met Amy’s eyes.

"What are you thinking, Flax?" Clover asked, clutching her necklace in her hands worriedly.

"She doesn't mean to destroy the palace door yet," he said. "We thought that's where she was heading."

"Then where is she going?"

They all stared at one another in tense silence.

A horrible crash like shattering glass cracked through the air. Amy found herself flying across the room. She rammed into someone against the far wall of the cavern. Shards of shattered crystal rained down around them. Disoriented, Amy vaguely realized that fairies around her were screaming and crying in terror as they fell to the ground.

CHAPTER TEN

The guard fairies by the crystal lily braced themselves, facing the wall near the entrance. It used to be a wall, anyway. Now it was just a smoking, gaping, crumbling hole.

One of the Guardians by the door had been cut by flying crystal. A trickle of blood oozed from the scratch on her cheek. Amy was surprised to see that the blood glistened silver in color.

Amy tried to push herself up and realized that she was lying on top of Flax and Clover. They'd been blown clear across the cavern by the explosion. Clover was already trying to scoot up onto her knees, and Flax was grimacing. His arm bore a row of shallow cuts from the shattered crystal.

"Flax, you're bleeding!"

He looked at his arm, then looked at her. "So are you," he said.

Amy could taste the blood in her mouth. Her bottom lip stung, and bright red drops were splashing to the white floor.

"Their blood really is red," Clover mumbled, looking at Amy and pushing herself up with a dazed expression.

The sounds of footsteps approaching echoed through the broken wall—a group was walking into the cavern.

"You need to get her out of here," Zinnia said, grabbing Flax. "Take her out the lower tunnel. She must not be found here!"

Flax's eyes flashed to the smoldering wreckage of the wall and then to Amy's bleeding mouth. He nodded and motioned for Amy to follow him as he started creeping away.

"Where are we going?" Amy asked.

"Shhh!" Flax hushed her. "Stay down and follow me," he whispered back.

"The queen is coming. You have to leave," Zinnia told her.

Clover curled up against the wall, whimpering.

Flax motioned urgently for Amy to follow him again, so she crawled over the shards of crystal, sharp as glass, along the wall where he was leading her. The shards cut painfully into her palms no matter how careful she was. Blood smeared among the shards of crystal over the white floor.

She was nearly around the back of the lily when the newcomers entered the cavern through the bashed-in wall. A tall fairy woman with reddish-brown hair strode in, flanked on either side by a dozen guards and servants. She wore a long, flowing white gown with deep-blue embroidery, and a shining, silver circlet rested on her brow.

If it wasn't obvious that this was Queen Orchid from what she wore, the way she carried herself as she walked into the cavern instantly told Amy that this fairy thought of herself as the one in charge.

The queen strode in with her entourage silently following behind until she reached the center of the cavern, right in front of the two fairies guarding the crystal lily. She regarded them mildly, like she was somewhat disappointed but not angry or even surprised.

The bleeding guards gripped their spears and braced themselves.

"Dahlia and Lantana, you were two of my most skilled royal guards, and here I find you actively working against me," the queen said. Her voice sounded smooth and musical. There was a rich resonance to it that made Amy's skin tingle, like she could feel magical power seething under the surface.

"Your Majesty!" one of them shouted desperately. "You must stop this. It's madness! The rowan trees won't grow in Titania! If you destroy the doors, we'll all die!"

Amy peeked around the side of the crystal lily and saw the queen's jaw tighten in response. She stared coldly at the guards. "We can grow anything in Titania. We just need proper motivation. Why should we be dependent on the human world? We have seeds, and water, and light, and good soil. The only reason our arborists refuse to rise to the challenge is because it's so easy to go through these doors and collect berries from mature trees."

"But, Your Majesty—" another fairy began.

"Silence! I'll not lose any more fairies to the hazards of the human world! We must cut all ties."

"All? But surely Your Majesty will at least leave the Titania Door . . ." Clover whimpered, still cowering on the floor.

Flax was waving frantically at Amy from a small tunnel hidden in the back wall. Reluctantly, she crept away from the giant crystal lily and crawled toward him, leaving streaks of red blood on the floor from her scraped palms.

"Even that one must be destroyed. It breaks my heart

to do it, but there is no other way," the queen said, in a softer voice than before.

"Please! My grandfather has died already, and my sister is so ill she can't leave her bed. You will doom us all if you destroy the last doors," a trembling voice cried from somewhere else in the cavern.

"And how many of us were harmed every day going through these doors in search of rowan berries?" the queen countered. "How many of you know someone who was permanently disfigured or killed by the humans' iron weapons? Or lost entirely to the temptations of the other world? No, it must stop. The only way to go from here is forward."

Amy was still crawling toward Flax, but her attention was transfixed on the queen and what was going on in the Crystal Cavern. Suddenly a warm hand wrapped around her mouth and forcefully dragged her into the cave. She tried to scream, but the hand muffled the sound.

"Shhh! Do you *want* to be captured?" Flax hissed in her ear.

"You scared me!" Amy hissed back, wrenching his hand away from her mouth.

"Come on, we have to get out of here before she sees you." Flax started crawling through the tunnel. It was more than large enough for them to stand and walk, but the entrance faced the cavern and they didn't want to risk having the queen look back and see them there.

"All right, I'm coming," Amy whispered. "I just wanted to see what was going on."

Behind them, fairies shrieked in fear. Amy felt a deep, reverberating boom pulse through the ground under her. A flash of light illuminated the tunnel for an instant, and then a shockwave crashed into them. Amy fell onto her face. She tried to get back up, but she was dizzy, and there was a high-pitched ringing in her ears.

She lay still for a moment, feeling like her body was glued to the floor, until the ringing quieted down and the dizziness started to fade away. She started hearing the crying and screaming coming from the cavern behind her again.

"What is this? Red blood?" The queen's musical voice pierced the air. "Who brought a human through the door?"

"N-no one, Your Majesty!"

"Don't lie to me; it doesn't work. There is a human here somewhere, at least one. How many humans came through this door?"

Someone was tugging at her arm. Amy looked up. It was Flax. He was standing now, pulling on her arm with a frantically worried expression. He didn't say anything, but it was clear that she needed to get up and run.

With great effort, Amy pushed herself to her feet and raced after Flax through the tunnel.

"This is bad. This is very bad," he said when they'd gone far enough that Amy couldn't hear what was going on behind them anymore.

"She thinks I came in through that door, though," Amy said, panting. "At least she doesn't know about *your* door."

"No, you don't understand," Flax said, taking her hand and leading her around a dark corner. "The queen can tell when someone is lying. It's part of her magic. So if they say that no one came through that door, she'll know it's true. And then she'll know that there has to be another one somewhere!"

Flax barely slowed as they took another turn and started heading downhill again. They came to a little nook in the wall and Flax pushed her into it, squeezing in after her.

"What are you doing?" she asked.

"Shhh!"

Amy heard light footfalls echoing through the dark cave above them. The rock walls pressing into her back and sides were rough and scratched her skin. In front of her, Flax's wings pressed against her, and she could feel the warmth of his body and smell the sweet spicy scent of his skin.

"They had to come this way. The blood trail led right into this tunnel," a male voice echoed.

Amy's breath caught in her throat and her heart hammered harder against her ribs.

"This isn't just a tunnel. This is a labyrinth," another voice griped.

"So grab some glow moss and we'll search. The human couldn't have gone far."

The footfalls drew closer. Amy wanted to run; she pushed against Flax, but he pushed right back, pressing her firmly into the cold wall behind them.

A mote of cool white light shone through the thick darkness, bobbing and weaving and seeming to grow in size as it drew closer.

"This way is clear," one of the pursuers called.

"Over here, I found a spot of blood!" The voice was close, too close. He was on the path right outside their hiding place.

Amy squeezed her bleeding hands into fists. She should have been more careful. She should have known, after seeing the silver blood of the fairies, that her red blood would draw attention. She could have wiped it up, or scooted on her knees, or something! Now they were going to get caught and it was all her fault!

The guard was shining his glow moss in a wide ark, looking through all the little dead-end tunnels.

Flax took a deep breath, and Amy could feel his muscles relax against her.

The guard turned to face them, shining a small ball of glow moss into their crevice . . . and then he turned away as though he hadn't seen a thing.

Amy held perfectly still, scarcely daring to breathe, while the guard turned and walked farther down the tunnel.

Flax lifted his head and started breathing faster.

"What . . ." Amy started.

"Shh!" He pressed back again, pushing her into the rock.

A minute passed. And then another. The darkness and silence seemed to stretch on for hours. Then the footsteps returned. The queen's servant walked past them again. Amy noticed that Flax was strangely relaxed again as the guard passed by their hiding place.

They stayed still in their dark little alcove until all noises from above went silent, and even then, Flax made Amy stay put while he crept slowly out to investigate.

When he returned, he was carrying his handful of glow moss, and Amy could see that his face was somber.

"What is it?" she asked.

"They're gone," he answered, his voice hollow. She could see that his face was scratched and bleeding from the scrapes of flying crystal. "They're all gone.

The Crystal Cavern is empty and the door is destroyed."

Neither of them said anything for a moment. Amy didn't know what she could say. Nothing she could do would make this better. She knew she didn't really understand—couldn't understand—the importance of that doorway to the fairies. And why had they all left? Where had they gone?

"Come on. Follow me. We need to go deeper into the mountain."

Amy followed silently, the glow moss lighting their way.

CHAPTER ELEVEN

Flax led Amy through the tunnel down deeper into the ground. His somber mood gradually lightened as he told her stories of adventures he'd had exploring these caves when he was younger.

They passed under a faintly glowing natural archway, and when they came to the other side, Amy caught her breath in amazement. They emerged into an immense cave with high ceilings. The walkway they were traveling on wound down past shallow pools of white water. Stalagmites and stalactites stretched from floor to ceiling like ornamental pillars, and glow moss grew everywhere, illuminating everything in clear blue light.

"Pretty neat, huh?" Flax asked.

"It's beautiful," Amy said breathlessly.

"This is one of the places glow moss grows naturally." He put his glow moss down near a pool and used his stone knife to scrape together a fresh ball that shone brighter.

"You don't use candles or lamps?"

Flax shrugged. "We don't use fire as often as humans do. For working silver and gold and for cooking it's great, but we don't do those things frequently. Cooking is usually for medicine or special occasions, and metalwork is for jewelry or armor. Besides, why would we even want to use candles when glow moss and glow bugs are so easily found?"

Amy shrugged and followed him down the walkway between the pools of still water and around a stone wall.

Everywhere she looked, Amy saw new wondrous things lit up by the glow moss—natural stone arches, pillars, and waterfalls. Glow moss, shining through pools, cast bright ripples onto the ceiling above them.

They passed through another corridor that opened up to an enormous cavern. At first, Amy wondered if they had finally made it outside. The ground under her feet was rocky and damp, and she could see no ceiling above them even though glow moss grew brightly on the wall behind her. In front of them, an open expanse of water gently rippled against the stones and light glistened across tiny waves as far as Amy could see into the darkness beyond. It looked like they were standing on a beach on a starless night.

"Is this a lake?" she asked.

"Yep," Flax said, carrying his ball of glow moss over to a row of white canoes tethered to the shore. There were several empty posts, making Amy wonder if there were missing canoes, and if so, who had taken them.

"An underground lake?" She looked out onto the water, shimmering almost as still as glass. "Is this the Mirror Pool?"

"No, no. Not at all. The Mirror Pool is in the Selva Wood, far east of here," Flax said, unwinding a rope from one of the posts, freeing a canoe. "Hop on in."

"I didn't know fairies liked boats so much," Amy said, hesitating. She didn't see any other side to this water. No light or noise or anything. As far as she could tell, they would be paddling into empty blackness.

"We do prefer boating to swimming," Flax noted. "The water weighs our wings down."

Amy laid her hand on the smooth wood. Flax wouldn't be getting in if they were paddling into nothing. She swallowed her fear and climbed aboard.

As soon as she was settled in her seat, Flax pushed

them off the shore and hopped in himself, picking up an oar and paddling them away from land.

Amy watched as the blue light from the glow moss faded farther and farther away. Finally, it was so dim she couldn't make it out at all.

"Are you sure you know which way to go? I can't see anything anymore."

"I'm pretty sure. My father took me through here once and showed me which cave leads out to the surface. As long as we end up on the other side of the water, we should be in the right place."

Flax fell silent and turned his face away.

Amy watched him for a moment. He looked so sad. "Your father . . . he's not—"

"He was taken to the prison a few months ago." Flax said. He took a breath and shook his head, like he was trying to shake off his somber mood. "He was the one who organized all of us to help the princess defend the doors. My mother and I, we've been doing our best to fill his role since. But she's looking after everyone in Lake Village and little Acorn as well. And I . . . well, I'm still pretty young, so I'm not exactly a powerful fairy."

The water rippling past the sides of the boat sparkled in the light from Flax's glow moss. Amy dipped her sore, scraped hands in and sighed with relief as the cold water washed away the dry blood and soothed the shallow scratches in her palms.

She thought about what Flax had told her. His father had been taken from him, just as she feared her own father would be taken from her. True, it wasn't exactly the same, but she felt like she understood him a little better now. And maybe he had understood her all along as well.

As Flax pushed the water with his oar, he seemed to be trying to fight a grimace of pain with the effort. Amy remembered that he'd been cut by the broken crystal as well, and his injured wing might also still be bothering him.

"Um, do you want me to help you paddle?" she offered.

"Well . . . okay, yeah. There's another paddle under your seat. If you work on both sides evenly, I can steer us from back here."

Amy fumbled around the floor of the canoe until she found the oar, and then she crawled back up onto her wooden seat and sank the paddle into the water. It was a lot harder than it looked. She'd never been in a canoe before, let alone helped paddle one.

Flax explained how to hold the neck of the oar in one hand and grab the grip with the other and how deep to sink the blade into the water. The smooth wood irritated the cuts in Amy's hands, and half the time she still got it wrong and only managed to splash herself and Flax with water.

Flax laughed while he tried to compensate for her erratic paddling with his own efforts.

Even with Amy's less than skillful attempts, they managed to pick up speed. She could feel a slight breeze in her face as the canoe cut quickly through the water toward the opposite shore.

"Look up ahead," Flax said.

Amy looked and saw what he was pointing out. A faint and familiar blue light was glowing at water level in the distance.

"Glow moss?" she asked.

"It's the other side of the lake. We're almost there."

"Then where do we go?"

"More caves for a while, unfortunately," Flax said, with a touch of chagrin in his voice. "Then we'll be on the other side of Mt. Oberon and we can make our way down to Tuleris."

"What's Tuleris?"

"The royal city," he said, matter-of-factly. "Actually, it's the only city. We have villages and towns, but Tuleris is our one great towering city. That's where the royal palace is."

"That's where Princess Lily is going," Amy whispered to herself. Once they were there, she could ask the princess to help her. Soon, she would be back at the farmhouse, and first thing in the morning, she would beg her grandmother to take her back to the hospital. She'd rush in and use the magic, and he'd be better. He'd jump out of the hospital bed and give her a real proper hug. They'd laugh and dance together. The doctors might try to stop him, but they wouldn't need doctors anymore. They'd run down the hallway together and escape that horrible place.

The blue glow got bigger and brighter as they paddled until Amy could see that the glow moss grew in a swirling pattern leading into a cave that headed uphill through the rock.

The bow of their canoe crunched up onto the shore. Flax hopped out, splashing into the water, and hurried to grab the rope and tie it off.

Amy followed him, pulling the rope and helping him wrap it around the nearest post to keep it from drifting away.

"Thanks," Flax said, taking the rope from her and tying it off in a very particular-looking knot.

Amy nodded and followed him through the swirling patterns of glow moss into the bright blue corridor.

The tunnel had a well-worn smooth floor, but the

walls were rough and rocky. Patches of glow moss shimmered and seemed to sparkle with light all around them as they passed near. The path slanted slightly up away from the lake and gradually widened until there was space for Flax and Amy to walk side by side.

A warm, delicious breeze blew over them, smelling of apple blossoms in springtime. Amy closed her eyes and breathed it in deeply. "Do you smell that?"

"Yes!" Flax said, and he started to walk faster. Amy had to hurry to keep up with him.

The rocky tunnel rounded a bend, widening even further, and Amy found herself running out of an ordinary-looking cave onto a smooth, grassy hillside bathed in moonlight.

Majestic trees once again surrounded them, and their tops seemed to stretch all the way up to the sky. The glow of moonlight sparkled off their bark, like they were dusted with glitter. Fireflies danced around the bushes in the undergrowth.

Amy crouched down and pressed her burning palms into the cool, dew-covered grass. It felt wonderful.

Flax sighed with relief and sat down next to her. "I don't like being in the tunnels," he confessed. "They are beautiful, but it always feels like I'm trapped in there."

Amy nodded. "I can understand that. I felt the same

way, especially when that guard was walking past us. I wanted to run, but it felt like we were cornered." She lifted her hands to examine the scrapes and cuts on her palms. Rows of angry red lines crisscrossed every which way through her skin. It was worse than she'd thought.

"I had to use some magic to help us out," Flax confessed. "Invisibility is a handy trick for those of us who travel in the human world, but here, not many fairies know it, so he wasn't expecting it. Are you all right?"

Amy was still frowning at her palms. "It was my fault that they knew where to look. I bled all over the floor and left a trail."

Flax scooted closer and looked at her palms. "Hmm, that won't do . . ."

"Maybe we can make some bandages?"

Flax shook his head. "I wouldn't want to risk it. Since you're with me and my wing is injured, it almost makes sense that you're walking everywhere, but you don't quite look like a fairy, and you have to hide the fact that you don't have wings. Having to hide red-colored cuts just adds one more risk to the pile. No, I need to do something about it. It'll take more magic than I was expecting to use, but I have enough now."

Flax took her hands in his, covering them with his

own, and then he closed his eyes and took a deep breath, concentrating.

Amy felt a tingle of energy in her palms. The tingle grew into a thrill and surge of power that shivered through her whole body. She felt the energy echo inside of her, somewhere near her heart, like whatever it was Flax was doing bounced around against something similar, but not the same, at her core.

Her palms warmed, and it felt like something soft and smooth was oozing over her skin. Then it stopped and Flax released her, looking weary but satisfied.

Amy held up her hands, wiggling her fingers experimentally. The tingling sensation was still fading away, but her hands were whole again. The cuts and scrapes had vanished.

"You healed them!" Amy gasped.

"Yeah . . . it was harder than I thought." He sighed deeply. "But it's for the best."

"Did you use all your magic again?"

Flax chuckled and stood, brushing the grass from his seat. "No, not even close. The elixir will recharge me to full strength. But I still need to be careful how much magic I use; it wouldn't do to waste it. Now, how am I going to get us down the mountain to Tuleris . . ."

Amy stood and tried to look down the hill through the steep peaks that surrounded them. She couldn't see anything that looked like civilization, let alone a city. "How far is Tuleris from here?"

"Very far, still. If I used more magic to heal my wing, I might be able to fly us there, but me having an injured wing is a handy excuse for why you don't fly. So leaving it injured is useful. But . . ." He turned to her with a growing smile. "I might know who can help us."

"Who?"

"They're usually on this side of the hill this time of night," Flax noted obscurely. "Stay very still and don't frighten them. They don't trust strangers easily."

"Okay." Amy wrapped her arms around herself, wondering who Flax's mysterious, shy friend might be.

Flax put both his index fingers in the corners of his mouth and blew a long, shrill note that rang through the trees and echoed over the hills.

Amy waited with bated breath to see what would happen.

Flax stood alertly, listening to the noises blowing in on the breeze.

Then Amy heard the faint beating of hooves tapping over the earth, and two graceful creatures, creamy white against the deep-blue night, pranced through the trees.

Their bodies seemed to glow. Their velvety sides rippled with powerful muscles. Their long legs danced over the ground with unconscious grace. Their sharp, cloven hooves struck the rocky ground without faltering. Their dark, soulful eyes twinkled with joy and wisdom, and each of their heads was crowned with a wide majestic rack of shining, white antlers.

"They're white deer!" Amy gasped, clutching her hands together in delight.

CHAPTER TWELVE

"They're *stags*," Flax corrected, walking toward one and rubbing its velvety nose with his hand. "White stags are among the most magical and intelligent creatures in the forest. These two are friends of mine."

Amy took a step closer, and the stag nearest to her shied away. The other snorted indignantly and tossed its head.

"Easy, Thistle. Settle down, Bracken. She's okay," Flax soothed. He stroked the neck of the other stag, and the beast lowered its head to nuzzle the fairy. Its impressive rack swung dangerously around Flax's head, but he didn't seem concerned.

"Bracken and Thistle?" Amy asked. She longed to go closer and stroke their lovely cream-colored sides, but she was afraid to startle them.

"Yeah." Flax smiled and shrugged. "I can't speak their language, and I don't know what they call each other, so I gave them fairy names."

"How are they going to help us get to the palace? You said they're magical—are they going to make a spell or something?"

Flax laughed again, but Amy couldn't tell if he was laughing at her question or because one of the stags was nibbling at his ear affectionately. "No, their magic is mostly concerned with escaping and hiding. They can use it to grant a single wish in exchange for freedom if they're captured, though."

"Then we should ask them for a wish!"

Flax frowned at her. "I would never do that to them. They would only use their magic that way to escape captivity. It would be cruel to trap them, and they would never trust me again."

Amy remembered how she'd felt in the caves, like she was walled in on all sides—like she would never be free again. She considered what it would mean to the stags if someone forced them into a situation like that to demand that they use their magic to grant a wish. "Oh, I see. No, we shouldn't do that."

"But, if they will allow it, we might ride them down the mountain. Bracken and Thistle are sure-footed and fast. We could get there very quickly with their help." He turned to the stags and spoke softly. "Bracken, Thistle, my friends, we need your help. This girl needs to get to the royal palace. Can you carry us there? It doesn't need to be all the way, just as close as you can."

The stags looked at each other and seemed to consider what Flax had asked. Then the one closest to Amy walked toward her, gazing at her intently. It stretched out its neck and sniffed her. Then it shook its antlers and twitched an ear, settling itself next to her as though waiting for her to climb on.

"Wow, that was a lot easier than I thought it would be," Flax said, running his hand over the muscular shoulder of the other stag. "White stags almost never let humans see them, let alone ride them." He narrowed his eyes at Amy. "It's almost like they trust you."

"Well, they can trust me." She reached out and stroked the neck of the stag in front of her. It was warm and even softer than she'd imagined. The beast turned his head to look at her with one dark sparkling eye.

"It must be because you're with me." Flax shrugged. "I've spent a lot of time with them, so they know I won't bring them to anyone dangerous."

He jumped up onto the back of his stag, throwing one leg over and settling himself into his seat. "You do know how to ride, don't you?"

Amy looked doubtfully at the smooth, white back of

the stag standing in front of her. She cautiously placed a hand on his side; his skin twitched, like he was trying to dislodge a biting fly, but he didn't move away.

"Well, I did ride a pony a few times. Kind of. We walked in a circle. And it had a saddle on."

Flax chuckled.

Amy could have sworn the stag's eyes twinkled brighter as it looked at her and twitched its ears.

"Here, let me give you a hand," Flax offered. He slid off his stag and walked over to her. "I'll help you up. And Bracken will take it easy on you, won't you, pal?" He patted the stag's shoulder. Bracken flicked his ears and tossed his head, waiting patiently for Amy to climb onto his back.

While Amy tried to scramble up the stag's smooth side, Flax put his hands under her knee and gave her a boost, shoving her up until she could swing her other foot over and settle in her seat.

Sitting on the big creature's back felt unsteady. There was nothing to hold on to, not even a mane like a horse would have. There were no stirrups to put her feet in, no saddle, no reins, and his soft skin slid around over his muscles as she moved, making it difficult for her to maintain a stable position.

Bracken shifted on his legs under her weight but didn't seem to mind carrying her. Then he shook his head and Amy leaned away from his wide, pointy antlers. If she moved her head too far forward at the wrong time, she could lose an eye on one of those deadly prongs!

She reached down tentatively and patted the smooth white neck in front of her. "Thank you, Bracken."

The stag twitched his ear and turned his head so one of his deep, intelligent eyes winked at her. Amy almost believed that they really could understand what she and Flax said. They were, after all, in a magical land. Maybe animals could understand speech here and Flax wasn't just pretending, the way people did with their pets.

"I really need to get to the palace to see the princess," she told him. "My father is very sick, but the princess might be able to help him."

Bracken snorted and lifted his head.

Ahead of them, Flax hopped onto Thistle's back again and started to ride down the hill.

Bracken turned his head further to nudge Amy's knee with his nose. Amy got the impression that the stag was trying to tell her something. Then he started following Thistle and Flax down the slope.

"He nudged my knee. What does that mean?" Amy asked. "Was he wishing me good luck?"

Bracken stepped down over some stones and Amy

almost lost her seat. She had to grip the little ridge between the stag's shoulders to stay on.

"He was telling you to hold on with your knees!" Flax called. "The trail down this side of the mountain is rocky."

Amy regained her seat and tried to hug Bracken's sides with her legs. It seemed to help a little, but she still wobbled to the right and left as they moved down the hill.

Ahead of her, Flax sat confidently on Thistle with perfectly straight posture. Amy felt a little jealous of his balance as she watched the stag and fairy move over the uneven ground together as one.

As they made their way steadily down the hillside, the deer tramped through beds of soft moss. Their hooves clicked and clacked over smooth stones. They pushed through clumps of soft bushes, scattering clouds of insects and startling small sleeping creatures under the brush.

Then Thistle suddenly stopped and lifted his head, stamping his forehoof and swiveling his ears forward as he stared up at the mountainside.

Bracken stopped too, following Thistle's gaze and staring alertly. Thistle wagged his tail nervously and huffed a loud breath through his nose.

"What is it?" Amy asked, looking around herself, sensing danger.

"Trouble is coming," Flax said, his voice low. "Not sure what it is yet, though."

Bracken's hide twitched under Amy's legs. She could feel his muscles tensing up underneath her.

Then Flax gasped. "It's the queen's guards! They must have known where the tunnel came out. We have to run!"

"What? I'll fall off!"

He turned to look at her, and Amy saw panic clearly written on Flax's face. "No time to argue. We have to go now!"

Without another word, Thistle bounded down the hill, and Amy just caught the humming sound of fairy wings from above before Bracken leaped forward as well.

The sudden jolt nearly threw her off the stag's back, but Amy crouched down and squeezed Bracken's neck while she gripped around his middle with her knees. Somehow she managed to stay on.

It took only a few seconds for Bracken to catch up to Flax and Thistle. Amy kept her eyes squeezed tightly shut, but she could hear the crashing sounds of both stags rushing through the thick undergrowth.

"Keep going! They can't fly after us through the trees," Flax called.

They took a sudden turn to the right and Amy slid down Bracken's side. She squealed in fear, trying to climb back up with her foot, but she only managed to slide lower.

Bracken didn't stop. He grunted, then gave a little jump, tossing Amy into the air.

For one horrifying second, Amy saw the ground rushing beneath her and a tree careening toward her head. Then she landed with a thump right in the center of Bracken's back. The stag grunted at her again. She regained her grip around his neck and squeezed with her legs, and Bracken put on a new burst of speed.

The stags raced down the hill. As they descended, the underbrush thinned, and Amy could see farther ahead between the trunks. The noise of their passage faded as their mounts no longer had to push through bushes and leaves as they ran. Amy noticed that she could hear the whir of fairy wings coming from somewhere above the canopy.

"They're still following us!" she cried.

"I know!" Flax shouted back. "We need to find somewhere to lose them."

The shouts and whirring from above drew even closer, and Amy caught a glimpse of a fairy guard in gleaming armor, wielding a sharp spear, searching through the gaps in the trees.

"Why don't they come down here?" she wondered aloud.

"We're going too fast for them. It wouldn't be safe to fly so fast through the trees, but that's not going to last much longer!" Flax called back.

Amy looked ahead and saw what he was talking about. The farther they went, the thinner the trees were getting, and soon they would disappear altogether. At the bottom of the hill, the forest opened up to a valley with sharp plateaus, large boulders, and shallow canyons scattered everywhere. Short grass blanketed the ground and bushes dotted the landscape. Ordinarily, it would be a delightful scene, somewhere Amy would like to bring a picnic lunch or go camping, but all she could think now was that they were about to lose their cover.

"What are the stags doing? We can't go out there; we'll be caught!"

"They can't run as fast uphill!" Flax hollered back. "We'll get caught if we turn around, too!"

Amy gripped tighter as Bracken hurdled a fallen log and barreled down the hill next to Thistle. Her arms were starting to feel numb from holding on so tightly. She could feel the stag's labored breathing through the muscles in his neck.

The stags raced out of the trees and into the open.

"There they are!" a fairy above them called. "After them!"

"Come on, faster!" Flax cried.

Somehow, they did manage to go faster. Running downhill must have slowed the stags down for some reason, because as soon as they were on the level plain, they picked up speed and flew over the ground.

The ride was much smoother now, too. Going downhill, every time the stags landed on their front hooves, their bodies had jolted forward making Amy feel like she was going to be thrown off. Now their motion smoothed out, like short, even waves of speed.

Amy relaxed her grip on Bracken's neck a little and dared to look up. The queen's guard fairies were flying after them from a distance, but not so far behind that she couldn't see the fierce expressions on their faces. One of them shook his spear threateningly.

Amy turned to watch ahead of them. The walls of low plateaus passed by them on either side in a whir. Bracken leapt over a low bush so smoothly that Amy would have hardly noticed if she hadn't seen it.

The guard fairies fell farther behind, too tired or perhaps too slow to keep up with the white stags.

They turned a corner into a ravine, still moving at a

blinding pace, when suddenly a musical noise sounded from ahead and above them.

"Oh no!" Flax moaned.

Both stags skidded to a halt as two more fairy guards flew over the ridge ahead. One of them was carrying a small white horn.

The stags reared and turned sharply to run back out of the ravine, but they hardly got to the corner before the first two guards flew into view, brandishing their spears.

CHAPTER THIRTEEN

The stags backed away from the guards nervously. They were both panting, and Amy could feel the heat and sweat coming off of Bracken's hide.

The four guard fairies loomed closer. The two that had been following them through the forest landed, folding their wings and breathing heavily.

"You're Flax, aren't you?" the fairy carrying the horn asked. "Hawthorne's son, right? We should have known. What did you do to these stags to make them carry you? And with a *human,* no less!"

Flax dismounted from Thistle and took a few steps toward the guard fairies. His face was red with indignation. "They're my friends! And you should know better than to chase them. Haven't you heard the legends?"

"If they don't want to be chased, then they shouldn't be helping fugitives escape," the guard fairy replied, pulling a thin piece of cord out of his pouch.

"Fugitives? Why are we fugitives? Is it *illegal* for a human to visit Titania? Or to give elixir to the sick?"

Bracken gave a little shake and Amy slid off his back, unable to hold on any more. Her arms throbbed and her legs wobbled under her before she collapsed into the dirt.

"You were consorting with rebel fairies who are known to oppose the crown," the guard answered, glaring at Flax.

"And you were clearly mistreating sacred beasts," one of the others accused, gesturing at the panting and sweaty stags.

Amy looked around their little alcove frantically. Was there a cave they could run into? Could Flax use his magic to help them?

Then she remembered the stags. They had magic, according to Flax. Powerful magic. Maybe they could help.

As one of the guards moved on Flax, grabbing him by the shoulders, Amy stumbled up to Bracken and draped her arm over his neck.

The majestic beast gazed at her. She thought his eyes

looked fearful. He gave a gentle grunt and blew warm air against her face.

"Bracken, we're trapped," she whispered. "We need to get out of here, but Flax and I can't fly. These other fairies are going to take us somewhere to be locked up forever. Flax said you two are his friends. Please, if you really are his friends, help us if you can."

The other guard was moving slowly toward Amy now, watching Thistle and Bracken with a large degree of fear and respect in his eyes.

"Why don't you come here, human girl?" he asked when he dared not approach any closer.

"No! Let Flax go and leave us alone!"

Next to her, Bracken stomped his hoof on the ground and snorted. The guard quailed and moved back a step.

"Don't be a coward," one of the other guards scoffed. "They're peaceful creatures. They won't hurt us." He brandished his spear and approached Bracken while two others moved on Thistle, forcing them back.

"Stop! Don't scare them!" Flax cried, struggling against the guard who was winding a thick cord around his wrists.

The stags stamped and snorted with wide eyes at the sight of the weapons trained on them. Thistle bellowed loudly and Bracken pranced back, knocking Amy to the ground.

Then both stags reared at once, bringing their hooves down on the rocks with a sharp crack.

The sound was unusually loud, hurting Amy's ears, like a boulder shattering into pieces. It echoed off the rocky walls and left a strange burning scent hanging in the air.

Amy blinked and realized that the guard fairies were nowhere to be seen.

Flax was on the ground, struggling to remove the cord from his wrists and grumbling under his breath.

"What happened?" Amy breathed.

"I'm not entirely sure," Flax said, ripping the last of the cord off and flinging it away.

Thistle approached and nuzzled Flax's shoulder.

Flax rubbed the stag's creamy white nose affectionately. "Thanks, pal. You two didn't have to do that."

"They used their magic for us," Amy said, finally understanding.

"It's strange," Flax mused. "The only magic they usually use is related to hiding and evading capture."

"They were trapped with us. So maybe they granted my wish." She ran her hand over Bracken's smooth neck. "Thank you," she whispered.

Bracken nuzzled her face.

When she looked up, Flax was watching her curiously.

"What?" she asked.

He shook his head. "I'm trying to figure you out, but I can't. You don't seem like a normal human to me."

"I don't see why. I'm obviously human." She patted Bracken's neck again, and the stag's eyes twinkled at her. She was starting to suspect that meant he was laughing.

They climbed onto the stags again and rode downhill through the valley. Running from the guard fairies had tired out the two stags, so they kept an easy pace over soft grass. After a few minutes, they paused by a little brook so they could all take a drink.

"What do you think happened to the guards?" Amy asked as they started on their way again. "Are they . . . gone?"

"Thistle and Bracken wouldn't hurt them," Flax assured her. "They either froze them in time or sent them far away. Maybe into the dragon kingdom!" His grin had a slightly wicked edge to it. "But no, probably not there, that would be too close to actually hurting them."

"Frozen in time? But they disappeared!"

"Yeah, and they might reappear in that exact same spot in a few days, wondering how the four of us suddenly vanished."

The stags plodded forward over beds of soft moss, and their hooves thumped on hard-packed earth. Flax and Amy grabbed handfuls of plump red berries as the stags waded through a field of bushes.

They traveled through another valley between two small hills. Small purple flowers grew all around them, filling the air with an unbearably sweet scent. Moonlight glistened off the dewdrops forming on the blossoms, making the whole valley look like it was sprinkled with tiny stars.

Then the forest returned, only these trees had smooth white trunks that stretched tall and thin into the sky. The rustling of their leaves overhead sounded like gentle rain. As they traveled forward, the soft sound was joined by another, deeper, rushing noise. The ground sloped down and they came to a swift river that was much too wide for the stags to jump across.

Bracken and Thistle stopped with a snort, staring at the water.

"Well, I think this is as far as they're going to take us," Flax said, sliding off Thistle's back. "The nearest ford is pretty far upstream and the nearest bridge is through Luna, and they won't go near a village."

"Then how are we going to get across?" Amy reluctantly slid off Bracken's back, eyeing the swift water.

"That's for us to figure out and not for these two to

concern themselves with," Flax told her. "Thank you, friends," Flax said, rubbing Thistle's nose.

"Thank you, Bracken," Amy said, swallowing her worry and stroking Bracken's neck. She had grown attached to the beautiful, gentle creature and would be sad to see him go.

Bracken slowly backed away from her. He solemnly lowered his head and closed his eyes, lifting one fore-hoof in a regal bow.

Then the two stags tossed their gleaming antlers and pranced back up the hill toward the mountains.

Amy watched them go, wondering at Bracken's bow. "That was strange. Is that their way of saying goodbye?" she asked.

Flax was staring after the stags with his head tilted and forehead wrinkled, looking perplexed. "Well . . . no. Not usually."

THE ROAR of the river filled the air around them as Amy watched Flax pace back and forth.

"Why don't we go down to Luna and use the bridge?" she asked.

"Because even though the stags could have gotten us there quickly, it's too far to walk. Also, it's well out of our way, and I don't want to risk anyone noticing that you're human unless we have to."

"Then we'll have to use the ford upstream."

Flax was already shaking his head before she finished speaking. "It would take forever to get there! And the ford is also much farther from Tuleris than we are now."

Amy huffed, frustrated. "Then we'll have to cross here!"

"Maybe a human can wade through that, but the current is too fast for me. I'd probably get swept off my feet."

Amy eyed the swift-moving water doubtfully. "Well . . . it's probably too fast for me, too," she admitted. "Do you think you can fly yet? Maybe you could carry a rope across and—"

Flax was shaking his head again. "It's only been a few hours, and it will probably take weeks for my wing to heal on its own. And I'm not going to waste magic on it unless it's absolutely necessary. Plus, you might end up drowning while I try to drag you through the water."

Amy huffed, feeling exasperated. "Well, I don't see another way for us to get across the river!"

Flax frowned thoughtfully, then crouched low by the riverbank, feeling the ground and looking across to the other side. "I think I have an idea. It will use some magic, but we don't have time to think of anything better." He stood, brushing the dirt from his hands.

"What are we going to do?" Amy asked, eyes widening at the thought of more magic.

"This." Flax held out his hand toward the far bank.

At first, Amy didn't notice anything happening. Then she heard the earth crunching and groaning around her. She looked around and saw the roots from the trees behind her stretching out of the ground like the tentacles of some sea creature, writhing and weaving together as they reached for the water.

On the far shore, more roots were erupting from the earth, wiggling and expanding into a thick twisted wooden cable.

Amy watched in awe as the two sides continued to grow toward each other. She saw the potential of what they might form and found herself internally encouraging the growth. She willed the roots to grow as they became thicker and stronger, widening and stretching, sending down anchors as they crossed the water. Finally they converged in the middle of the river, forming an uninterrupted arc over the rushing waves.

Vines crept in, twisting and weaving over the brown wood, adding green leaves and small white flowers. Amy watched the intertwining tendrils as they filled in all the little gaps between the roots. The vines continued spiraling around, just as she thought they should, sending out shoots and leaves and flowers until the wooden roots were completely covered up and she and Flax stood staring at a sturdy, arched, living bridge crossing over the water.

CHAPTER FOURTEEN

"Wow!" Amy gasped. "I didn't know you could do that!"

Flax took a shaky breath and let it out slowly. "How did that happen?" He glanced at his hands. "I made a whole bridge?"

"Isn't that what you were trying to do?"

Flax blinked at her. "Kind of. Not really. I mean, it takes less magic to grow plants than it does to heal, so I hoped I could at least get something sturdy enough for us to hold onto while we crossed..." He smiled at her and shrugged. "I must be stronger than I realized."

They set off together across the living bridge. Amy expected it to sag under their weight, but the roots were as sturdy as thick wooden planks. She peered over the edge into the river to see the bubbling choppy water underneath them. The rushing water was so clear, Amy could see the rocks trembling under the surface in the moonlight. Long, slender fish undulated smoothly, racing against the current to maintain their place in the river. There was no way she could have waded to the other side.

After crossing the river, their course wound through a warm valley and around a gentle hill. Amy was starting to wonder if they would ever make it to the city on time, but Flax assured her that they were almost there.

"As soon as we get around this bend, you'll be able to see the Tuleris," he said.

"Will there be a lot of fairies there?" Amy asked as the bubbling and splashing noise of the river faded behind them.

"Yes, Tuleris is the center of our civilization. Most fairies live in small villages scattered throughout Titania, but Tuleris is a big city. It surrounds the royal palace and is much bigger than any village."

"So . . . if there will be so many fairies . . . how will we get through without being caught?"

He nodded grimly. "We will have to figure out how to get in and find the princess without you being noticed. There are many fairies in Tuleris who would fight for the queen . . . even though she's dooming us all." He turned, saw Amy's concerned expression, and put on a confident smile. "But I think we'll have better luck there than in the Crystal Cavern. Nobody in Tuleris will suspect that you're human at a glance. You should blend in enough. And, besides, most of them will be asleep at this time of night."

Amy didn't trust his optimism, but she nodded in agreement. What other choice did they have?

"Why are any fairies on the queen's side at all?" she grumbled. "If you all need the elixir from rowan berries to live, and she's destroying your only way to get them, I don't get why anyone would fight for her to begin with."

Flax took a deep breath, stretching out his wings. Amy marveled at the iridescent colors that flashed through his wing membranes before he closed them against his back again.

"Because she's the rightful queen." He sighed. "She's the firstborn of the two sisters, and Princess Lily is hesitant to challenge her for the throne."

"But . . . why? Would they have to duel in a fight to the death or something?" Amy thought she remembered reading something like that in a storybook once.

Flax gave her a strange look. "Humans are so morbid

sometimes," he mumbled. "No, it's not a fight to the death. But it does have serious consequences for the loser. Still, I'm sure she would win. She would make a much better queen than Orchid."

"But if it isn't a fight, what would she be afraid of? What could keep her from saving everyone? Doesn't she care that you're all running out of elixir?"

"Of course she cares!" Flax snapped, scowling at her like she'd just insulted his mother. "But the consequence of losing the challenge . . . well, it might as well be death for a fairy."

"What do you mean? You said it wasn't a fight."

Flax pulled on the cord hanging from his neck and drew his blue pendant up so Amy could look at it. She noticed two wavy lines, like waves, etched into the stone with a circular shape above them that resembled a rising sun or moon. "This is a talisman. Every fairy has one. Our parents make them for us when we're born and they stay with us our whole lives. The talismans focus our magic and direct spells. Without this, I could barely do any magic at all. I would still be alive, but I'd be dependent on others for basic, simple things like getting in and out of restricted buildings, or healing, or making elixir. I would be as helpless as I was when you first found me . . . but all the time."

He shuddered at the thought and dropped the talisman against his chest.

"In order to challenge Orchid for the throne, Princess Lily would have to risk her talisman. There's a pedestal in the throne room made by Queen Titania over a thousand years ago so that there would never be conflict over who should rule. Anyone in the royal family can put a talisman on the pedestal. If the pedestal accepts it, that fairy's magic becomes tied to the land instead of the talisman, firmly establishing that fairy as our ruler. But if the pedestal rejects it, the talisman is destroyed forever."

"Kind of like the sword in the stone," Amy said.

Flax shot her a knowing look. "That's right, only a bit more dramatic."

"So neither of them have tried the pedestal? How can Queen Orchid rule, then?"

"She doesn't need to try the pedestal. She's queen by birth. The pedestal is only there for when there is a conflict. And, so far, Princess Lily has been trying to reason with her sister, not challenge her."

As they came around the last bend in the hill, Amy finally saw the city down below them. The valley they were walking through led to a dirt trail. Farther down, the trail opened up to a road. The road led farther on, up a gentle slope, and into the shining city of Tuleris. It didn't look like any city Amy had ever seen. There were bridges and houses and mansions with tall spires. But there were also enormous trees that glowed with rainbows of light from hundreds of windows up and down their trunks and along their branches. At the crest of the city sat a white palace that shone in the pale moonlight. It had dozens of towers and long streaming banners that fluttered in the night breeze.

"Wow, that's so amazing!" She glanced at Flax, worried that maybe he wouldn't appreciate the beauty of the fairy city as she did. This place was a source of so much heartache for him, maybe it would trouble him to even be near it. But her friend's eyes shone with joy and admiration as he looked out on the palace and glowing, towering trees.

"Come on," he said, hurrying down the trail. "Princess Lily should be somewhere in the city. We'll need to ask around, but we should be able to find her soon."

There weren't many others traveling the road to Tuleris so late at night, but they did pass a merchant with a small pony drawing his cart away from the city. He watched Flax and Amy curiously as they walked past him. When his eyes fell on Flax's bandaged wing, that seemed to satisfy him.

"Most fairies would fly into the city from here," Flax

whispered to her as soon as they were out of earshot. “Unless they're carrying heavy loads. That’s one reason I didn’t want to bother using magic to heal my wing.” He adjusted Amy's cloak to help it billow out at her back and make it look more like she had wings hidden underneath.

The road led them through the outskirts of the city. They were surrounded by small earth houses nestled between smooth tree trunks. The trees also had windows glowing from them and even little stone chimneys poking out here and there, smoking happily and casting spicy-sweet smells through the air. It was like a town and a forest merged into one.

They came to another river over which a long, narrow bridge stretched toward the outer rampart of Tuleris. Golden lanterns hung from the parapets along the bridge at regular intervals, lighting the way for them.

More fairies strolled along the bridge or fluttered through the air around them. They looked like they were intent on their own business and uninterested in two young fairies walking toward the city together, but Amy stayed as close to Flax as she could, afraid that someone would notice her at any moment.

Flax took her hand, and his warm, comforting touch helped her relax a little.

They reached the other side of the bridge and walked through the tall wooden gate into the city. Towering spires, arches, and more enormous trees immediately surrounded them. Fairies fluttered everywhere, filling the air with shimmering wings in every color of the rainbow, some in subdued browns and grays, others in flashy reds, yellows, or stripes of black.

Flax led them straight up the main road and around a bend. Amy's eyes widened when the large archway that led into the palace came into view. This was it. This was where the Titania Door was—where Princess Lily would be!

"Psst! Flax! Over here!" A low voice hissed from the side of the road. Both Flax and Amy turned to see an old fairy with white hair and powdery wings beckoning to them from an entryway in a nearby tree. She was bent with age and seemed weary, but her eyes were sharp and urgent as she waved them over.

Flax squeezed Amy's hand and drew her along with him toward the tree. The old fairy ducked inside and they followed her, finding themselves in a warm room bathed in orange light from a handful of lanterns. Fairy men and women sat at small tables situated throughout the room, eating and drinking but looking generally morose. Amy wondered if this was some kind of restaurant. It was a cheerless one, if so.

"Back here," the old fairy said, leading Flax and Amy behind the counter and down a short hallway to an empty room.

"What is it, Camellia?" Flax asked, as soon as they were alone. "Do you have any word of where the princess is?"

Camellia looked at Amy closely and then nodded. "So, it's true, you did bring a human child here. Is it also true that the queen destroyed the door in the Crystal Cavern?"

Flax's shoulders sagged and he nodded. "Yes, she did, only a few hours ago. We were there."

Camellia frowned and shook her head. "And the Mirror Pool has been destroyed, too. Did you hear?"

"Yes. I heard." Flax's voice came out in a low growl. "She wasn't supposed to be there. We thought she was looking in the southwest."

"There is only one door left," Camellia said, her eyes downcast. "And that door doesn't lead to rowan trees anymore. We're out of options. Out of hope."

Amy glanced at Flax, wondering if he would tell Camellia about his secret door, but he only stared at the wood floor under his feet, deep in thought.

"How did you manage to bring the human through the door anyway?" Camellia asked, raising her eyebrows at Amy. “That takes a lot more magic than you’re capable of.”

Flax flushed and shook his head, as though shaking himself out of a disturbing thought. “It’s a long story, but I need to take her to the princess. And she needs to be sent home before the last door is destroyed.”

Amy blinked in surprise. She hadn’t been thinking about why she needed to see the princess at all; she’d been more concerned with the problems the fairies we’re facing. She remembered Flax’s little brother, Acorn, crying desperately and greedily drinking the elixir when it was ready. What was going to happen to him if all the doors were gone?

"The princess is waiting for her sister near the southern dance court. She’s gathering forces there to defend the last door.”

Flax nodded. "Then we'd better be on our way. There's no time to waste. Thank you, Camellia, for the information."

Camellia frowned and stayed in her seat. "Don't thank me. I've done nothing to be thanked for. I just told you what I know."

Flax stood and took Amy's hand. "Come on, Amy. We can get there quickly. You can ask for the princess’s help and then we need to send you home before you're stuck here for good."

Amy bit her lip in concern as Flax led her out of the room, through the hallway, and toward the sitting area. Then they stopped short.

The open area was nearly empty; all the fairies who had been sitting and eating at the tables were gone.

Blocking the entryway, glaring fiercely down at them and surrounded by her guards, stood Queen Orchid.

CHAPTER FIFTEEN

Flax froze and pushed Amy behind him. He still held her hand, and she could feel him trembling in front of her. His wings fluttered in frantic little bursts, brushing against her arms.

"So, you're Flax, the underage berry hunter, human snatcher, and son of the rebel leader. Don't you know that it's a crime to bring outsiders to Tuleris uninvited?"

Amy saw Flax's jaw tighten when the queen mentioned his father, but he didn't answer; he just glanced around the room as though searching for a way to escape.

"Your father is already in my prison, but it appears that you didn't learn from his mistakes, did you? We can't have you running around and causing mischief, so, unfortunately, you will be joining him until we decide what to do with you."

"No, you can't send him to prison!" Amy protested, trying to push Flax aside so she could glare at the queen.

Queen Orchid ignored her, gesturing to two of her guards. The burly fairies rushed forward and pinned Flax's arms to his sides, strapping his wings to his back with a thin cord to prevent him from trying to fly away. Flax cried out in pain as they tightened the cord around his wings.

"Stop it! You're hurting him! Can't you see that he has an injured wing?" Amy yelled. She tried to fling herself at them and fight them off, but two more guards grabbed her and pulled her forward so that she was standing right in front of the fairy queen.

"And you . . . a little human girl." Queen Orchid gazed down at Amy curiously, ignoring the struggling sounds of Flax being bound by the guards. "How did you come to be in my domain? This little imp is much too weak to have brought you through the door. It must have been one of the mature rebels who did it. Why did they bring you here? They must have had a purpose."

Amy was about to shout at the queen that she'd brought herself here and the Guardians had nothing to do with it, but she hesitated. If she told the queen how she'd really come into Titania, the queen would have all kinds of new questions for her. Then how would she keep from revealing the truth about Flax's secret door?

According to Flax, the queen had magic truth-reading abilities. If Amy lied, the queen would know.

"I . . . I really don't know how I got here," she said, keeping her eyes on the floor. She hoped that answer was truthful enough to satisfy the evil queen.

Queen Orchid gazed at Amy for a silent moment. Then she reached out a long smooth finger and raised Amy's chin so she was looking into the queen's face. "Surely, someone must have told you why you came here . . ." She raised her lovely eyebrows inquiringly.

Amy gulped and licked her lips nervously. Her heart was hammering erratically in her chest. "N-no. Nobody said they wanted me here for any particular reason."

The queen's brow furrowed, puzzled. She released Amy's chin and looked at the guards who were holding onto Amy's arms. "Bring the girl as well."

Amy didn't bother trying to resist as the guards bound her wrists behind her back and led her and Flax toward the exit. Many fairies crowded the street outside the tree, watching in curious silence, murmuring to one another as Amy and Flax were dragged into view. Amy thought she heard one or two of them whisper, "Oh no, not Flax!"

As they were being dragged out into the road a voice

wailed from the arched entryway to the tree behind them. "I'm sorry! I had to!"

Amy turned her head to see Camellia standing just inside the tree, wiping tears from her eyes with a cloth and staring plaintively at Flax. "It's my great-granddaughter Ivy! She's so ill. And she's only a tiny little one! She hasn't woken in days. The queen promised me elixir if I helped her. I'm sorry, Flax! I had no choice!" Camellia broke down in sobs.

Flax turned away from her with a sad sigh.

As the queen took her place at the head of the procession, Amy noticed one of the guards toss a small cloth bag to Camellia. The old fairy caught it in her hand and looked at it with a strange mixture of relief and disgust on her face.

The guards took their positions around the queen with Amy and Flax near the back. Standing between two guards in front of Amy, Flax looked dejected with his head slumped down.

"We are finished here," Queen Orchid announced. "These prisoners are to be taken to the palace. I suspect the girl might be important to the rebels for some reason, so she is coming with me. I'll not risk them setting her free. The imp goes to the prison with the rest of them."

A guard dressed in gleaming silver-and-blue armor answered the queen with a bow. "Yes, Your Majesty."

Amy was barely paying attention to what the queen was saying. All around them, staying at a respectful distance, fairies were watching. Some were peeking out of windows or hovering just within view. A few of them seemed to recognize Flax. These covered their mouths or gasped in horror at seeing him in the queen's custody. A couple of them seemed to realize that Amy was not a fairy. They stared and pointed, whispering to one another.

Suddenly, Amy's guards gripped her arms firmly and lifted her off the ground. Then, with a rush of wind, all the fairies beat their wings sending a gust over her face and blowing fallen leaves, dust, and flower petals into the air. Together they lifted off and soared into the air, veering up the hill toward the royal palace.

If Amy hadn't been so terrified, she would have been delighted with the flight. The cool air higher up felt marvelous as it blew on her face and neck and through her red hair. The fairy city below looked wondrous and magical with shining trees caressed in moonlight, warm glowing windows, and dancing fireflies peeking out of dark corners. Best of all, the royal palace, stretching up into the heavens, looked like the most fantastic castle in every little girl's fairytale dreams. There were tall smooth towers with pointed peaks, shining banners fluttering in the breeze, arches, turrets, and a wide courtyard with an enormous sparkling fountain in the center.

They flew over the outer rampart and a delicious fragrance floated up toward them, probably carried on the breeze from the royal kitchen. Amy couldn't tell exactly what the smell was, but it reminded her of apple blossoms and chocolate.

Their flight path took them between rows of graceful turrets on which fairy guards stood post, carrying longbows and quivers full of arrows with gleaming sharp tips.

As they approached the main building, the guards who were carrying Flax veered off to the left and started flying down toward a low stone outbuilding with dark narrow windows.

"Wait! Where are you taking him?" Amy cried, struggling against the stretchy rope that bound her hands and writhing in the arms of her guards.

"He's being taken to the prison, young lady," one of her guards reminded her. "They aren't going to hurt him."

"But we need to stay together."

"Your friend is a known enemy of the crown," the other guard said, gruffly.

"Flax didn't do anything wrong. He's been helping people!"

The guards didn't answer her. They set their faces and carried her straight ahead, following the queen.

They flew through a large, wide archway into the most breathtaking room that Amy had ever seen. Twinkling lanterns lined the outside wall they had flown through. Intricate tapestries hung from the opposite wall, showing scenes of fairy life through all the seasons of the year. Dancing in the sunshine of spring. Harvesting and juicing fruits in the fall. Gathering to make music with exotic instruments in the summer. Roasting nuts around a warm fire in the winter. In the middle of the far wall, a gigantic fireplace sat empty; only ash-blackened stone showed where winter fires had once burned. The white marble of the mantle was carved with vine and flower shapes. The ceiling above them looked like silver tree branches weaving their way through thousands of tiny panes of colored glass. It was difficult to see the colors of the glass in the darkness of night, but it still looked beautiful. Below them, blue, white, and yellow marble covered the floor in an enormous patterned mosaic. At the far end of the room, a raised dais held a white wooden table and gracefully carved chairs.

"This place is beautiful," Amy said breathlessly, looking around with wide eyes.

"It should be," the queen answered. Her musical voice echoed in the huge empty room. "This is the great hall of the fairy queen. This is where we hold winter festivities, have dances, and entertain guests."

The queen dismissed her guards with a casual wave of her hand. Most of them flew out the large opening in the wall. Two of them remained, standing near the queen with stern but detached expressions. These seemed to be the queen's personal bodyguards. Amy wondered if they thought she would try to hurt Queen Orchid somehow.

The queen took Amy by the arm, gently but firmly, and led her toward the dais at the far end of the room. Her guards followed silently behind them.

Amy looked all around, hoping to see some sign of hope, some way out. Maybe one of the guards was really on her side. When she glanced back, they continued staring forward, ignoring her.

She wondered about Flax, too. They'd taken him to the prison. Would he be able to figure out a way to escape? Probably not. The queen had said that all the "rebels" were being held there. If none of them had managed to get out, how could Flax?

Queen Orchid took Amy through a hallway to the

right of the dais into an anteroom just beyond. From there, more arched passageways led to several other rooms.

The queen walked past the first two rooms and gestured her hand to the third, looking down at Amy. "This was my own bedchamber when I was young. It is one of the most secure rooms in the entire palace. Only someone of royal blood can unlock the barrier to enter or allow anyone in. I'm sure you will be most comfortable in here. There will be no escaping this room for you once you enter unless I personally allow you through the door. Not even the captain of my guard will be able to release you without me being present."

"But there isn't a door," Amy said, looking through the perfectly empty archway into the fairy bedchamber.

"Not a physical door," the queen said. "Haven't you noticed that none of our buildings have doors? Fairies detest feeling trapped, so we secure our homes and fortresses with magic rather than material. It's more effective anyway. Show her, Bryony."

The fairy guard next to Amy reached out his hand toward the empty-looking opening. There was a slight humming sound as his hand met some invisible resistance. He pushed his hand forward, but it didn't budge. The space where his fingers met the boundary started to shine with bright white light.

"And if the intruder persists, there are consequences," the queen said, her voice dark and ominous. "Take it further, Bryony."

The guard looked at her with trepidation. Then he licked his lips and pushed his hand into the invisible barrier. There was a sudden loud crack, a flash of blinding light, and Bryony fell back, grimacing and shaking his hand like it had been stung.

"Now, will you tell me what you know about the rebellion?" the queen asked, staring down at her coldly.

Amy hesitated, looking from the queen to the hapless guard who was grimacing and shaking out his hand. The fingers that had been zapped seemed to be limp and lifeless.

"If you do me this favor, perhaps I might do something for you in return," the queen said in a gently persuasive voice.

Amy looked up at her. "What do you mean?"

"Fairies and humans have an ancient bond of cooperation. True, there has been mischief on both sides, but when it comes to something important, we can form pacts to help one another.

"Up until today, I believed that I was on the verge of completing my mission. All I had to do to seal us off from the human world was to close the last two doors forever. But then I find you here. I don't know what to make of you, and that concerns me. I want to know what the rebels were planning to do with you, and I think you know more than you say.

"If you tell me everything you know about the rebels and what they're planning, then I agree to grant you one wish, anything within my power. It will be the final pact between humanity and fairies in all history. Isn't that a magnificent thought?"

Amy swallowed and felt her hands trembling at her sides.

The fairy queen was offering to grant her a wish, anything within her power. Queen Orchid obviously had the power to save Amy's father. She was probably the most powerful fairy in Titania. If Amy told her everything, if she explained that her father was dying and that all she wanted was magic to cure him, she could get that magic and go home immediately. She only had to tell Queen Orchid about Flax's door and she could be back at her grandmother's house right away.

CHAPTER SIXTEEN

Amy took a calming breath as she considered the queen's offer.

Queen Orchid could give Amy magic to heal her father. It was what she had been hoping for. It was the whole reason she came to Titania in the first place.

But if she told the queen about Flax's secret door, she would surely destroy it the moment Amy was on the other side. Flax would still be in prison. Then where would his family get rowan berries to make elixir? Where would *any* fairy get berries for elixir anymore? What would become of them all?

Amy looked away from the queen as a tear trickled down her cheek. She couldn't do it. She felt sick to her stomach for not agreeing immediately, but she thought of Flax's baby brother, Acorn. She thought of how weak and ill Bromeliad had been in the Crystal Cavern. She even thought of Camellia crying over her great-granddaughter, willing to do anything to save her life. She couldn't lead the queen to the last door the fairies could use to survive just so it could be destroyed.

"I don't have anything to tell you," she mumbled.

Queen Orchid was silent for a moment. "I see," she finally answered in a cold voice. "Then you will be spending a lot of time in this room until you can remember."

Amy bit her trembling lower lip and watched as the queen reached for a gold chain hanging from her neck and drew a milky-white talisman out of her robe.

Amy blinked, astonished at how familiar the queen's talisman looked. It seemed almost identical to the necklace Amy was wearing under her dress at that very moment.

Queen Orchid held her talisman up to a spiraled mark on the wall near the archway and motioned for Amy to enter the bedchamber. When Amy stepped inside, the queen tucked her talisman back into her robe.

"Now," she announced, narrowing her eyes at Amy, "I must deal with my troublesome little sister. Whatever this is, it reeks of her work. Once I've discovered the reason you're here and neutralized whatever threat you present, I'll be able to destroy the final door and cut our ties to the barbaric human world forever."

She turned sharply to her guards. Bryony was still nursing his sore hand, but he stood straight as soon as the queen's gaze fell on him. "Collect all the duty guards. My sister is bound to be in the city somewhere. We will find her and deal with her and whatever plan she had with this human, and then we can finish the work tonight."

"Yes, Your Majesty," they responded in unison.

She turned on her heel, stalked gracefully through the anteroom, and disappeared through a large archway followed silently by her two guards.

Amy watched them until they were out of sight, then turned to examine her prison. Perhaps there would be something in the room that could help her.

There were blue-velvet bed curtains and plush blankets draped over the mattress, and cushions sat in piles around the floor. On a small vanity desk there was a silver mirror, a basin of cool water, and a smooth white comb. Shelves lining the walls were filled with books written in a strange language she couldn't read. Nothing looked particularly useful to her.

She went to the small window and poked her head outside, trying to figure out where she was in relation to the rest of the palace. Was she too far from the ground to climb out the window? Could she see the prison where Flax was being held?

She thought she recognized the wing of the palace to her right. Beyond that was a tall turret with a steep peak and a place where the rampart turned a corner toward the courtyard. If she remembered correctly, the prison was on the other side of that wing. If she could get out of this room, could she make it there on her own? Could she help him escape?

She swallowed nervously. It was her fault Flax had gotten captured in the first place. If he hadn't been helping her get to Princess Lily, he never would have been in the royal city to begin with. He never would have gotten captured. He would be free to go back through the door to her grandmother's barn as often as he needed to collect rowan berries for everyone in Titania.

She had to at least try to help him.

Amy walked back to the archway that led to the anteroom, approaching it nervously in case it decided to zap her if she got too close. As she looked closer, it didn't give any indication of wanting to harm her.

She ran her fingers around the carved frame, feeling the cool smoothness of the wood, and she noticed that the familiar symbol of a tree with splayed roots was carved in prominent, key places in the design; it looked like the same symbol that was on her necklace . . . and the queen's talisman.

Amy drew out her necklace. She looked closely at the tree carved on her pendant and at the one on the wall. They were perfectly identical. Every branch and every root was exactly the same. How could that be? Was her necklace somehow from Titania? It seemed somewhat possible, since there was a door to the land of the fairies in her grandmother's barn, but what did it mean? How did it end up in a box with her name on it?

The more pressing question was, would Amy be able to use her necklace the way the queen had used hers? Could she use it to get out of the room?

There was no swirled mark on the wall on Amy's side of the archway as there was on the outside. The queen had said something about someone needing to be from the royal bloodline, but if the talisman was like a key, and the key was only given to fairies within the royal family, wouldn't a key still work even if someone else found it? If Amy had somehow gotten her hands on a royal key, maybe it would still work for her, even though she was just a human.

She tried touching her necklace to the border around the archway. Nothing seemed to happen. So she stretched out a hand to test the barrier that was supposed to block her from escaping. She reached her fingers forward, farther and farther.

She didn't feel a thing.

If she was going to do this, she wanted to do it quickly. She didn't want to be halfway through and have the spell suddenly zap her whole body.

She took a few steps back and ran headlong at the archway. She squeezed her eyes shut and braced her shoulder, half expecting to meet solid resistance.

Instead, Amy found herself stumbling out into the anteroom, tripping over her feet, and landing with a huff on the floor by the far wall.

"Wow," she said, pushing her hair out of her face. It had actually worked! She'd gone right through the archway as though it was as empty as it looked.

She wondered if it had been a trick all along. Maybe Queen Orchid had been bluffing.

Amy stood and smoothed out her hair and dress. Now she needed to figure out which way to go if she was going to save Flax—back into the banquet hall where she'd come from or on into rooms and passages where she didn't know where she would end up?

If she went back the way she had come, it was possible that she might be able to find her way out of the great hall, sneak down to the ground level, and figure out how to get to the prison from there.

She hadn't seen any obvious way for a wingless human to get down from the great hall, though, and it was also going in the opposite direction from where she thought Flax was being held.

On the other hand, Queen Orchid had gone the other direction, through the palace and toward the prison. If Amy went that way, she might run into the queen and be captured again, and then she would be put somewhere she couldn't escape from. Toward the prison was the direction she needed to go, however, and it seemed like the most likely way to get down to the ground.

Amy bit her lip in anxiety, looking both ways. Finally, she turned toward the archway where Queen Orchid had gone and marched forward.

Amy had to get to Flax and help him out of prison. She owed it to him.

After that, they could find Princess Lily together and finally save her father.

CHAPTER SEVENTEEN

Amy tiptoed into the hallway where the queen had gone. Small golden lanterns illuminated the smooth curved white walls. The polished floor glistened in their light. Amy wondered if other fairies often came through there. If so, there was nowhere for her to hide, and she would surely be caught. If the royal guard or even a maid entered the hallway, they would see her for sure.

She tried to walk softly, keeping her footsteps as light as possible as she made her way down the long passage, but nobody came. All seemed quiet and still.

The hallway opened into another anteroom with multiple archways leading into larger rooms. Amy poked her head through the archways to see what was inside them.

The first room had a large desk with a velvety throne-like chair behind it. Rolled scrolls sat in a stack on the desk with a slender quill standing in an inkpot. There were sticks of dark-blue wax and a small stone carving that looked kind of like a tall chess pawn.

The next room was filled with a comfortable arrangement of chairs. A beautiful crystal chandelier sparkled from the ceiling, and an enormous harp stood near the window, gleaming in the moonlight.

The third archway led to a corridor. Along one side there were entrances to more rooms; along the other, large windows looked out onto the courtyard and buildings. Amy immediately recognized the row of narrow windows in the lower outbuilding—that's where they'd taken Flax!

She leaned out the nearest window, looking at the distant ground below her. How could she get down there? It was much too far to jump. There had to be stairs somewhere.

Then she stopped, realizing that there was no guarantee of stairs anywhere in this place. Fairies could usually fly anywhere they needed to go. Why would they bother to build stairs?

Fighting a sense of hopelessness, Amy followed the corridor, looking out every window that she passed, hoping for some clue to help her get out and down to the ground level. When she made it to the halfway point, a large opening led out to the open air. No stairs. No ladder. Nothing that she, a wingless human, could use to get down.

Amy heaved a sigh and continued walking. She was actually getting farther from the prison building now. With every step, she expected to be discovered and captured and stuck somewhere she would not be able to escape from.

Finally, the corridor turned a corner and Amy discovered stairs leading down through a narrow stone passage. The passage led farther into the palace and away from the prison. She peered down into the darkness below. At the bottom of the stairs, there was another sharp turn into a hidden room. She couldn't hear anything, but there did seem to be a soft orange flickering light coming from around the corner.

Well, she couldn't go back the way she came, and she couldn't jump out one of the windows, so this seemed to be her only option.

Amy made her way down the stairs, staying close to the wall so she would stay hidden until she actually rounded the corner at the bottom. She could hear her own breath echoing off the hard stones surrounding her, and it reminded her of traveling through the underground passageways with Flax. Had it really only been a few hours since they came through the tunnels? It felt like years.

When she got to the bottom, she peeked around the corner to see what was in the next room.

An enormous stone hearth filled the wall on the far side. The top of the lintel was taller than Amy was, and the inner hearth looked big enough to fit her grandmother's car inside completely. A lively fire burning within was what gave the flickering orange glow to the room. She could hear the flames crackling as they danced along the logs.

A long wooden table stretched across the floor with bowls of fruits, bundles of herbs, strings of garlic, roots, and nuts. Rows of small clay pots as well as stone knives and long cooking utensils sat on the wood surface in a neat, organized manner. The hot air in the room smelled of spices and pastries.

Amy realized that this must be the palace kitchen.

She crept around the corner, eyes wide and looking all around for anyone who might be hiding out of sight.

"And who might you be?"

Amy jumped and whirled around, heart sputtering in her chest.

She looked up to see who had spoken, and an old male fairy with short white hair fluttered down from the wall of shelved spices behind her. The sound of his wings was disguised by the low roaring of the fire, so Amy hadn't heard him hovering.

He flew lower and landed a few feet away. Amy saw that he was wearing an apron dusted with flour and carried a fistful of what looked like cinnamon sticks in his hand. "Well?" he asked, frowning at her. "Did you sneak in from outside? What is your name?"

"I . . . I, um . . ." Amy hesitated. This fairy thought she was one of them. If she told him her name, he would immediately be suspicious. Flax had commented that her human name was weird.

Only it wasn't, not really. Amy realized that her *full* name might pass for a fairy name. It was the name of a flower, after all. All the fairies she'd met—Flax, Marigold, Acorn, Zinnia, even Bromeliad—were named after plants.

"My name is Amaryllis," she said, grimacing, hoping she could pull this off.

The fairy narrowed his eyes at her. "Well, Amaryllis, my name is Chive, and it's my job to prepare food for Her Majesty and the palace staff. It is also my job to make sure no little imps come snooping in here to eat the strawberries and honey, got that?"

"I . . . I wasn't going to . . ." Amy stammered.

"Then why are you here? A forest pixie like you has no business in the royal palace."

"I . . . I just . . ." Amy had to think up a lie quickly. She had to come up with something that this fairy would believe—something that would be reason enough for a common fairy to risk sneaking into the royal palace. "My friend is ill," she said. "He needs elixir badly. If he doesn't get it soon, I'm afraid he'll die."

The old fairy's expression softened a little. "You came looking for elixir?"

Amy nodded, too frightened to look him in the eye. She kept her gaze on the cream-colored stone floor.

"And what makes you think I'd give it to you? Elixir is scarce all around these days. If I gave it to every beggar who asked for it, there wouldn't be any for the royal guard, the court, myself, or even the queen."

Amy nodded. "You're right. I should just leave." She tried to look sad as she turned to the large exit at the far end of the room that looked like it led outside.

She got a few steps down the room before Chive called out, "Wait just a minute!"

Amy froze in place and turned to look at him warily.

Chive gritted his teeth and rubbed his face in irritation. "Come on over here. Did you at least bring a satchel?"

Amy patted the pockets of her dress. "I have these."

Chive pressed his lips together uncertainly. "Be careful as you fly home, then. It wouldn't do to drop these; they break easily." He handed over five glass vials of glowing purple elixir.

Amy took them in trembling hands. "But, what about the staff . . . the guards . . . the queen?"

He shook his head. "We all get more regular rations than anybody else. It sounds like your friend needs this a lot more than I do now. Just don't go telling anyone where you got it, understand?"

Amy swallowed nervously and slid the vials carefully into her pocket. "Thank you," she whispered.

"Now go on," he said, gruffly, shooing her away with an impatient wave of his hand. "Get out of here and go help your friend."

Amy nodded gratefully, then turned and hurried out the door.

She found herself running out into the wide-open courtyard. The large marble fountain that she'd seen from the air spouted sparkling streams from the center of the wide space. Rows of tall swaying trees stood between the walls of the palace and the fountain on either side. Their leaves whispered together as the night breeze rustled through them. Small groups of fairies walked here and there, talking to one another in quiet voices that Amy couldn't hear over the rushing sound of the fountain. Now and then a fairy would open his or her wings and take off in a gust of swirling wind.

There weren't many places for her to hide. She would have to walk from the kitchen to the end of the palace wall in the open.

Amy wrapped the traveling cloak around her body and pulled her hood up over her red hair. She hoped that this would help her blend into the shadows a bit.

She was pretty sure the prison was off to the left, somewhere around the corner of the palace wall. She started walking ahead, keeping an even pace and trying to casually stay out of the way of the fairies milling about. She kept her head down, not looking at anyone and trying to seem like a boring and forgettable fairy, not a human prisoner escaping the queen.

The palace wall led her past the fountain and away from the activity of the fairies in the courtyard. Slowly, the sound of splashing water, low voices, and whirring wings faded behind her. The light from glowing lamps and lanterns receded as she moved farther away, and darkness enveloped her.

She came to the end of the wall, turned the corner, and there it was.

The low stone building with narrow windows sat in a darkened space in an abandoned corner of the palace grounds. Amy instantly recognized it as the building where the guards had taken Flax. She could see the entrance from where she stood, and there didn't seem to be any guard posted. Amy looked all around for anyone who might catch her. She even searched the sky and the ramparts above, remembering how the cook in the kitchen had caught her because he was flying. No fairies were anywhere near. She guessed that they must avoid this unpleasant place. Or maybe there was a law against lingering nearby.

Whatever the reason, Amy still didn't want to take any chances. There wasn't anyone there to see her now, but someone might come around the corner or fly overhead at any moment. She followed the narrow shadow along the outer palace wall, getting as close to the prison building as she could. Then she stopped when she couldn't get any closer without leaving the shadow. She had to cross an open lawn to get to the building now. There were no trees or bushes or anything to hide behind.

She looked around once more. The windows and archways in the palace behind her seemed to be empty. None of the fairies from the courtyard had followed her. There were some guards on the ramparts and towers above the prison, but they seemed to be looking outward, watching for visitors or intruders coming in, not for a prison break happening behind them.

She stepped away from the wall and walked out of the shadow. Her feet sank into the thick moss blanketing the lawn as she rushed forward. A slight breeze made her cloak flutter around her body and she pulled it tighter, hoping that it would hide her from any searching eyes.

Her whole body was trembling with fear. What if someone was watching her right now? What if she couldn't get in? What if Flax wasn't there? What if she was wrong and this wasn't the prison after all?

She finally made it to the prison wall, reaching out to touch the rough grey stones, making sure they were real.

She wondered where in that building Flax was being held. She didn't dare call out to see if he would answer from one of the windows, as there might be guards patrolling inside, ready to capture anyone who tried to cause trouble. Instead, she followed the wall to where she'd seen the large dark archway.

Just like the passage leading to the queen's childhood bedchamber where Amy had been imprisoned, the entrance to the building didn't have a physical door; there was just an empty space leading to the darkness within. Strange symbols were carved into the stones all along the vertical supports and into the curved top of the archway. At the very tip, engraved into the keystone, Amy saw the familiar symbol of the tree with splayed roots.

CHAPTER EIGHTEEN

Amy hesitated, biting her lip nervously, before trying to pass through the archway. The symbols around the supports looked a lot like the ones that had been around the bedchamber entrance. Since there wasn't any kind of real door there, it made sense that there might be a powerful spell blocking anyone from going in or leaving.

Also, if the guards weren't outside the building, they must be waiting inside. Would they catch her as soon as she tried to go in?

She would have to risk it. She couldn't stay outside the prison forever dithering about what to do.

Amy reached out with her fingers to test the entrance.

Her hand stopped partway through, like the darkness was pushing back against her. She drew her hand back and rubbed her fingers. She didn't want to test the barrier any more than that, not after seeing how it had shocked the fairy guard back at the palace.

She frowned, looking around. Maybe there was a window big enough for her to crawl through.

Then her eyes fell on one of the marks on the archway. It was the same swirling design that was outside her room in the palace. The queen had used her talisman on it to open the entrance so Amy could go in.

Amy pulled her necklace out from under her dress. The golden chain sparkled in the moonlight. The engraved tree design looked exactly like the one on the keystone at the top of the archway. The creamy white pendant shone in the faint moonlight.

If what she carried really was one of the fairy talismans, and it was powerful enough to allow her to pass through a barrier that blocked even the royal guard, was it possible that it could unlock this one, too?

She held the talisman in her hand and pressed it to the spiraled mark in the stone archway, willing it to work.

Nothing seemed to happen. Amy reached her hand out again, testing the barrier, and this time she didn't feel any resistance at all. Her hand passed through as though nothing had ever been there to stop her.

Amy sighed in relief and walked through the archway, tucking her necklace back under her dress.

She paused inside the entrance to check for any guards, but the inside of the prison was pitch black, even darker than the lawn outside. The arch led to a hallway that stretched right to left. She could make out the far wall opposite the entrance, but the darkness closed in quickly beyond that.

Soft shuffling sounds came from somewhere inside. Was a guard coming? Amy backed into the wall and held her breath, listening.

Something protruded from the wall behind her, poking into her back. It felt like a hard wooden bar or lever.

She waited a few more seconds, but the shuffling sounds seemed to be coming from the prison cells, not the hallway, and no guard had called out. She moved away from the uncomfortable thing in the wall and turned around to see what it was.

It was a smooth wooden stick, about the length of her arm, nestled in some kind of holster. Could it be a magical key to unlock the cells? Amy grabbed it.

The moment she took it from the holster, the end of the stick burst into golden light that flooded the hallway around her.

Amy gasped and dropped the stick like it had

burned her. It clattered loudly on the stone floor. Now her eyes were so dazzled by the flash of light, she couldn't see anything but the colorful spots burned into her retinas.

"Who's out there?" called a tired voice from one of the cells. Whoever it was had to be one of the prisoners. "Is that you, Firethorn? I thought you went home for the night."

So, the guard had gone home for the night? Or maybe Firethorn was their caretaker. It didn't seem like fairies put guards on prisoners. They trusted their barrier spells too much.

"I'm not Firethorn," Amy called back.

Rustling sounds came from several more cells, like people crawling over dusty floors. The prisoners were getting up to listen.

Amy hesitated, unsure of what she should say next. She didn't know what would happen if she gave away that she was human, but her full name seemed to work with the royal chef.

"I'm . . . My name is Amaryllis. Does anyone know which cell my friend Flax is in?"

"Amy? Is that really you? It can't be!" Flax's familiar voice cried from the end of the dark aisle.

Amy reached down and grabbed the light stick. Again, it burst into light, and Amy directed it away from the archway behind her, hoping that no one would notice it and come rushing in to catch them.

She hurried down the wide stone hallway, past cell after small, cramped cell. Some of them were empty, but sad, weak faces peered out of others watching her pass. Fairies huddled in corners hugging their knees or lay in piles of straw and moss. None of them looked too healthy.

When she got to the end of the row, Flax was waiting for her just inside the entrance to his cell. "How did you find me?" he asked, his whole face lit up with joy at seeing her. "How did you get in here? Did one of the guards let you in?"

Amy shook her head. "The guards went with the queen. I was alone in the palace, so I snuck out. I don't think there's a guard here now, so come with me!"

Flax frowned, looking at the rim of the archway. "I can't get out of here. It's enchanted." He held out his blue talisman, which glowed faintly in the darkness. "I don't have the authority to unlock the barrier." He looked at Amy, wrinkling his forehead curiously. "There should be a barrier on the entrance to this building, too. How did you manage to get past it?"

"Oh, it must be this." Amy pulled out her necklace and showed it to Flax. She noticed that it, too, seemed to be glowing faintly.

Flax's eyes widened. His mouth fell open. He stepped back nervously and pointed at the necklace with a shaking finger. "How did you get hold of that? Did you meet the princess? Did she give it to you?" He gulped and whispered, "Did you steal it from the queen?"

"No! It's mine. Or it was my mother's. My grandma says she probably left it for me when I was a baby. But look." Amy pressed her talisman to the spiraled mark on the side of the arch, reached into the cell to grab Flax's hand, and pulled him out into the hallway with her.

"It seems to work just the same." She grinned at him.

Flax was staring at her with a half-terrified, half-bewildered expression.

"What?" she asked, starting to feel self-conscious under his stare.

"Who *are* you?"

CHAPTER NINETEEN

Amy's nerves were already stretched to the breaking point. She didn't want to deal with any more mysteries or drama or weird questions.

"What do you mean, *who am I?*" She scoffed. "You know who I am—the girl who saved your neck when you were stuck in my grandma's barn, and I'm the girl who's saving your neck again right now."

"But . . ." He looked at her necklace and back at her in amazement.

From down the hallway they could hear one of the other fairies coughing and moaning.

"I don't understand it any better than you do," Amy told him, "but we don't have time to figure it out now. We need to get out of here."

Flax shook his head, squeezing his eyes shut. "You're

right. Now is the time to escape." He looked at Amy. "We need to get the others out. They won't last much longer if we don't. Can you help?"

Amy nodded. "Yeah, I think I can get them all out. But, Flax, I heard the queen say she was going to destroy the Titania door tonight. We need to hurry!"

Flax looked toward the palace, eyes wide with concern. "Right!"

Together, they ran down all the rows of cells, checking for prisoners trapped within. Amy paused at each occupied room long enough to open the enchanted barrier while Flax helped the weakest prisoners get out into the hallway.

"Why aren't there any guards here?" Amy asked. "This is a prison, right? Shouldn't there be someone watching to make sure the prisoners don't escape?"

"The enchantment is so powerful, nobody has ever been able to escape before. Even if you broke down the walls, the magic barriers would still stop you," Flax answered. "At least, that's how it was until you came. Only a guard with authority granted from the queen or the princess could set the prisoners free."

"Wait, if the princess could set you all free, why doesn't she?" Amy asked, unlocking another cell with a young female fairy trapped within.

"Princess Lily has always wanted to teach Queen

Orchid to be a fair and just queen. She doesn't want to start a war." Amy thought she could hear disappointment in Flax's tone. "She sends elixir to the prisoners when she can, but if she came and released everyone, it would mean that she's openly working against her sister. Then Queen Orchid would retaliate, and that would start everyone fighting."

Flax helped an old fairy out of the next cell and Amy realized that she recognized this one. "Bromeliad!" She gasped.

Bromeliad nodded and grimaced as he lowered himself to the ground. "Yeah, it's me. I didn't stay hidden long enough after the destruction of the Crystal Cavern. Her Majesty caught me as I was trying to sneak out."

"Are the others here, too?" Flax asked. "Zinnia? Daisy? Rosewood?"

"Yes, I think so." Bromeliad sighed. "You don't happen to have any elixir on you by chance, do you? My cellmate, Yarrow, is nearing the end."

Flax shook his head sadly. "I gave it all away."

"Wait a minute!" Amy said. "I have some here." She reached into her pocket and pulled out the five glass vials of elixir that Chive had given her in the kitchen. "I got these from the palace chef while I was escaping," she explained. "He thought I was just a fairy looking for elixir to save a friend."

"Wow, you are full of surprises, aren't you?" Flax said, grinning at her. "Let me take those and you can go set everyone else free."

Amy handed over the vials of glowing elixir, then ran off down the hallways, looking for the last of the prisoners.

She pressed her pendant to the magical lock on every archway she came across, poking her head in to check for unfortunate victims. Usually there was a fairy or two trapped inside. Sometimes the cells were empty. Occasionally, the prisoners were too weak and ill to get out on their own.

As she was making her return trip back up the last row of cells, Amy found a male fairy with shaggy black hair who was too weak to stand anymore. He lay on the dusty floor, leaning against the cold stone wall and gazed up at her with eyes that seemed to see nothing.

Amy walked over and draped his arm over her shoulder to help him stand, but he was too weak to make any attempt and she wasn't strong enough to lift him on her own.

She rushed back out into the hall where the freed prisoners were talking and embracing one another, rejoicing in their new freedom. Flax was administering small doses of elixir to the fairies who needed it the most.

"Flax, I need your help!"

Flax immediately rushed over to follow her into the last cell. When he looked in and saw the ill fairy, he cried out in alarm and ran over to him. "Father!"

Amy stood and watched as her friend pulled out one of the vials of elixir and tipped it into his father's mouth. The fairy swallowed weakly, then took a deep breath. "Flax? How did you get here? Were you captured?"

"Yes, Father." Flax smiled and almost laughed with relief. Amy saw a shining tear trickle down his cheek. "But it's all right. My friend is helping us to escape."

"Friend? Escape?" The older fairy blinked his eyes and made an effort to sit up.

Flax gestured to the entry where Amy stood. "My friend, Amaryllis. She prefers to go by Amy, though. She's a human girl, come from the other side of the door." He smiled at Amy. "This is my father, Hawthorne."

Hawthorne eyed Amy with the first spark of life she'd seen since Flax had given him the elixir. "A human girl? But how?"

"I'm not sure." Amy shrugged, holding her pendant in her hand and fiddling with the chain. "I seem to be able to open fairy doors and unlock enchanted barriers."

"That's not so important right now," Flax said. "Amy

says the queen is going to destroy the Titania Door tonight. We need to protect it!"

Hawthorne ripped his eyes away from Amy to stare at Flax in alarm, then nodded and let his son help him stand on unsteady legs.

"Actually," Amy interjected, "I think she said she was going to find her sister first to make sure she wouldn't get in the way. It seemed like she thought me being here was part of Princess Lily's plan. She wants to destroy the last door after she gets the princess out of the way."

"I see," Hawthorne said. "Then we don't have a moment to lose. We must get to the princess before Queen Orchid does and warn her. Then we must protect the Titania Door at all cost."

All the fairies gathered together in the hallway by the light of the magic torch to organize their escape. Hawthorne and the other weakened fairies were quickly regaining their strength after taking some of the elixir. They were all animatedly discussing potential plans of action. Some wanted to move on the palace, since they were so close already. Others wanted to regroup with the rest of the Guardians in a nearby village.

"We must get to the market court," Hawthorne announced as he approached them. "We have reason to believe that Orchid is seeking out Princess Lily, and that is where she will be now. Who has strength enough to help the human girl?"

There was a startled murmur among the crowd as dozens of eyes stared at Amy.

"Yeah, I forgot to mention that I'm human." Amy grinned sheepishly and waved a hand at them. "Also, if we're flying, Flax might need help, too. He hurt his wing in my grandmother's barn."

Hawthorne gave his son a sharp look. Flax grimaced apologetically and shrugged, waving his bandaged wing. "I fell onto some farm equipment," he explained.

Four fairies volunteered to help carry Amy and Flax.

Moments later, they stood grouped around the exit as Amy pressed her pendant to the arch. The prisoners poured out onto the lawn and took off, heading through the dark corner of the palace grounds. Many of them looked at Amy curiously as they passed, glancing at her pendant, but none of them made any comment.

Amy and the fairies who'd agreed to escort her were the last to leave the prison. When everyone else had made it out safely, Amy slipped through the door and stepped out into the night. The fairies took her arms firmly and lifted off with a whir of wings and a rush of wind.

They flew swiftly, keeping low to the ground and staying out of the light coming from the lamps and palace windows. Their flight path took them around the palace wall and under a small grove of trees, and it ended where the fortified wall met a splendid garden filled with hundreds of sleepy flowers, willowy trees, and carved statues of fantastic beasts and heroic characters. At the base of the wall, a small creek flowed into a pond of cool clear water shining in the moonlight. Some plants nearby were giving off the most luscious scent Amy had ever smelled. If they hadn't been on such urgent business, she would have loved to curl up and sleep in that garden under one of the fragrant bushes.

Hawthorne and a few of the other fairies waded into the pond, and Amy noticed that they were working on a small, circular gate set into the wall that let the pond water flow freely out of the garden. They got it loose and pulled it away, letting everyone pass through to the other side.

"Come on, Amy," Flax whispered, grabbing her hand and pulling her along after him.

They joined the group, stepping into the water carefully so they wouldn't splash, and Amy picked up her skirts to keep them dry as they waded through the water under the wall.

Once they were on the other side, everyone started moving very fast. Someone grabbed Amy around the middle and lifted her, and then they were swarming, flying swiftly over the buildings and through the trees, headed down the hill to the lower houses and the roads lined with shops all dark and closed for the night.

Then they dropped, descending in a steep dive that made Amy's stomach flip inside her and clutch the fairy's arms around her waist.

They swooped toward the ground, leveling off and flying into a wide covered area lit by many bright lanterns and filled with wooden tables and chairs.

A crowd of fairies was already gathered to one side. They turned in alarm, bracing for conflict as the new fairies joined them. When they noticed who was coming, several ran forward, arms wide and smiling in welcome.

They landed, and Amy was released. The two groups of fairies collided with shouts of joy and laughter. Looking around, Amy recognized Zinnia from the Crystal Cavern hugging a fairy that looked like she might be her sister. Bromeliad was speaking with a small fairy who looked younger than Flax, patting his head and nodding solemnly. She recognized a few of the other fairies as well, though she didn't know their names. Everyone was smiling and rejoicing in the reunion.

A warm hand clasped hers and pulled her forward.

She looked and saw Flax, grinning at her as he dragged her through the crowd.

"What?" she asked, blinking in surprise and nearly tripping over her own feet as she tried to keep up.

"Come on! Follow me!" he shouted over the commotion.

Ahead of them, the crowd parted and Amy saw Hawthorne and a few other fairies speaking together. Hawthorne turned his eyes on Flax and Amy and smiled. "Ah, and here comes our little savior. She presents quite an enigma. I don't know what to make of her."

Hawthorne turned aside as the crowd parted some more, and Amy finally saw the fairy maiden he was speaking to.

She had bright red hair that cascaded down to her waist in gentle spirals. Her wings, which she kept tucked behind her back, shimmered in a rainbow of colors. Her light-blue gown flowed around her graceful form like a waterfall, matching the color of her eyes in the lamplight exactly. On her brow, she wore a gold and silver circlet that seemed to shine brighter than the lamplight allowed.

She looked at Amy and her lips parted in surprise; her slender hand went to her throat and she gasped.

This must be Princess Lily; there was no one else it could be.

Heart hammering in her chest, Amy did her best to bow respectfully. "Your Highness, I'm honored to meet you."

The princess came forward and cupped Amy's chin in her soft hand, lifting her face. Amy saw tears glistening in her eyes. "Child, you do not bow to me."

CHAPTER TWENTY

Amy gulped nervously. Had she done something wrong by bowing to the princess? She didn't want to offend fairy royalty.

"Oh, sorry. I don't really know the right way to meet a fairy princess. I'm just a human girl," Amy mumbled lamely.

Princess Lily laughed, a gentle musical sound. "There is nothing to apologize for. This is quite a turn of events for us. I understand that you probably have some questions about how you managed to enter Titania and free my friends from prison."

"You mean . . . you know how I did that? Was the queen right and I'm a part of your secret plan?"

"Not in the way she thinks. Come, sit with me and I'll tell you everything." The princess turned to walk toward a table removed from the crowd that offered a little privacy.

"Wait! I mean . . . please, Your Highness. Your sister is looking for you. She's on her way to stop you."

Princess Lily turned back with a small smile. "My power is greater than she knows. Orchid won't soon find us here. But we will be as brief as we can. I don't like leaving the Titania Door unguarded, knowing what she intends to do." She looked in the direction of the palace with a sad expression.

"Well, um, okay." Amy joined her at the simple wooden table, sitting in a creaky chair and fiddling with a lock of her red hair.

"Now, how about we start at the beginning, shall we?" Princess Lily asked, taking her seat so gracefully that it might as well have been a royal throne.

"Okay, I guess you want to know why I came here."

The princess cocked her head curiously. "You . . . wanted to meet *me,* didn't you?"

Amy was starting to feel very nervous and extremely insignificant. Here she was, barging into a fairy civil war that could kill their whole society just so she could ask for a favor. Even if that favor was to help save her father, what was that in comparison to the lives of everyone here?

But she couldn't back out now. She'd come all this

way and finally found the princess. If she didn't at least ask, she would never forgive herself. "I did come through the door to find you. Flax told me that you might be the only fairy powerful enough to help me."

Now the princess looked concerned. "What do you need help with?"

Amy didn't dare look at the princess as she spoke, afraid she would read rejection in her expression. "I need . . . I was hoping you could give me some magic to save my father. He's very ill. The doctors think he won't live much longer. They've tried everything, but he keeps getting worse. Magic is the only thing that can save him now."

The fairy gasped softly, and Amy finally looked up. Princess Lily had her hand to her mouth and an expression of horror on her face. "Brandon is dying?"

Amy stared at her, bewildered. "That's my father's name—Brandon. How did you know that?"

Princess Lily took a deep breath and lowered her hands to the table. "I can see that you don't understand as much as I presumed you did. I should explain my side of the story."

"Okay . . ."

"Fifteen years ago, I was feeling trapped and stifled living at the palace. I felt I had nothing important to do and no purpose. I was fascinated with tales of the human world that I read in the royal library, so, eventually, I ran away and created my own door to the human world. I suspect you know of this door—tucked under a tree next to a river west of Lake Village?"

Amy nodded, waiting for more.

"While I was there, I met a young man named Brandon who loved to sit under the rowan tree by the barn and play music on his guitar. I was hesitant at first to even let him know I was there, but after some time he convinced me that I could trust him. We eventually became friends. I helped him with his songs and he answered all my questions about the human world, telling me such fascinating things I couldn't help coming back for more.

"At the time, life in Titania seemed dreadfully dull while life in the human world was full of adventure and love. I felt I had no significant obligation to Titania—my sister was queen after all—so I abandoned my kingdom to marry a human man and live among their kind forever."

Amy's eyes grew wide. She could hardly believe what she was hearing, but she still wanted to hear it all. She didn't dare speak. Her throat felt too tight to speak now anyway.

"I spent three wonderful years married to a man I loved dearly, but when we were expecting our first child, an emissary from Tuleris came through the door and sought me out. She warned me that my sister considered my actions to be rebellious. It was an affront to the crown, the royal family, and all fairykind. She had often spoken of cutting off Titania from the human world before. It was a topic we'd argued about regularly. After my defection, she decided to finally act and put an end to travel between our worlds forever.

"Even though my sister has convinced herself that the reason rowan trees don't grow in Titania is because our arborists are lazy or don't understand the species, I knew that this would mean a slow and agonizing end for my people."

She stopped and looked down at her hands clasped in her lap.

"I had to come back, if only to talk some sense into Orchid. I couldn't stand idly by while my people died senseless deaths." She looked back up at Amy. "It broke my heart to leave, but I had to. I'm sorry I wasn't there for you all this time."

"That means . . . you're my mother?"

"That's right." Princess Lily smiled.

"But . . . why did I never know about this? Why didn't my father tell me?"

The princess shook her head. Lamplight glinted off her royal circlet. "I don't know, but I'm sure he had his reasons. I had planned to tell you everything when you were old enough to understand."

Amy blinked away tears, looking up at the fairy princess—her mother—and feeling more hopeful than she had dared before. "Then, you'll help save him? You'll use your magic to cure my father?"

Princess Lily smiled and let out a short laugh that sounded almost like a sob. The moisture in her eyes spilled over into glistening tears that trailed down her cheeks. She rose from her chair and knelt before Amy, then took her in her arms and embraced her softly.

"Of course I will! Of course! We will go to him together and I will cure him."

"Together? You're going with me?" Amy smiled.

"I must. I can't cure him otherwise. I have to go to him with my talisman and use a powerful healing spell. It will banish all disease from his body."

"So you're going to bring your talisman to my father and use a spell to cure him? I thought you'd give me something to take to him."

"I'm afraid there's nothing I can give you that you can use yourself. Once I'm sure Titania is safe, we'll go together and I will cure whatever illness he has."

"But why can't it be a potion or something I can take to him right away?"

Princess Lily shook her head and clasped her

talisman in her hand. "That would take time. I don't know what ails him. And even if I did, it would take more time, days or weeks perhaps, to brew the correct potion. No, it would be much faster and more effective for me to go personally. Besides"—she smiled at Amy and stroked her cheek with the back of her hand—"I've missed you both so much. I want to see him again."

"So, is that how Amy was able to unlock the door?" Flax asked as they walked up one of the side streets toward the palace.

They were on their way to the throne room, where the Titania Door was, to confront Orchid and prevent her from destroying it. Princess Lily had enchanted the back streets leading toward the palace to conceal their approach so they could come upon the palace without alerting Orchid. If the queen knew they were on their way, she might rush to finish the job immediately.

They were making their way through narrow walkways between smaller buildings, sales carts covered and stored for the night, the backside of buildings, and trees where fairies lived. In the human world, this kind of street would be in disrepair and lined with dumpsters, but in the royal city of Titania, even the most humble streets shone with magic and beauty.

"Yes. She should be able to go through the door with no effort at all. I designed the barrier to unlock for my blood signature so it would not deplete my magic to make frequent trips through it. That means it should open for my children as well."

Flax's wings buzzed in surprise. He seemed reluctant to leave Amy's side even though he'd already held up his side of their bargain. Since Amy was walking alongside her mother, he was joining in their conversations, too. "You made a door to the human world and a lineage barrier spell at the same time? I didn't know that was even possible!"

Princess Lily laughed. "Well, it certainly wasn't easy."

"I don't understand," Amy said. "There are different kinds of barriers?"

"Yes, there are many kinds. Most are standard barriers that don't allow any living thing to pass without permission. Some only work against animals. Others only work against fairies. Most of the doors between the worlds are meant to keep humans and iron out, though any fairy can temporarily open them with enough magic. But there are barrier spells that will open for anyone within a bloodline. In the palace, for example, many of the doors don't allow anyone to pass unless they are descendants of Queen Titania and King Oberon."

"Oh, maybe that's how I got out of the bedchamber!"

Princess Lily raised an eyebrow at her inquiringly.

"Um . . . Queen Orchid put me in her old bedchamber instead of the prison. She thought I was important to the Guardians somehow and figured I couldn't be rescued if I was there."

The princess nodded thoughtfully. "If you had been anyone other than my daughter, that plan would have worked, but because you're of the royal bloodline yourself, you can go virtually anywhere in the palace without obstruction."

The road ended at a smooth lawn surrounding the outer rampart of the palace, and their whole party stopped, looking up at the wall. Several pairs of eyes turned to Princess Lily.

"We will have to cross over here," she announced.

"But, Your Highness, the guards!" Hawthorne protested.

"Let them see us. There are fewer on these towers than over the main gate. It will take longer for them to respond. If we hurry, we should be in the throne room before Orchid can react."

They organized into several smaller groups. Princess Lily insisted that Amy be carried by two of her most trusted bodyguards. Hawthorne, of course, agreed to carry Flax.

At Princess Lily's signal, they took off and shot toward the wall. They picked up speed so quickly, Amy felt like she'd left her stomach behind on the ground somewhere.

At first, the guards pacing behind the balustrade didn't seem to notice them. Perhaps it took a while for the concealment charm the princess had put on the road to lose effect. Then, as they gained altitude and started crossing the wall, the guards turned in sudden alarm.

"Go directly to the throne room. Don't attempt to engage with them!" Hawthorne shouted.

The guards were already bringing shining horns to their lips and sounding loud, clear notes that echoed across the stone walls of the palace.

The Guardians put on a new burst of speed, zooming between two tall towers, over a long, low wing of the palace, and over a dark sleepy grove of fruit trees. Then they swung around and Amy saw the familiar sight of the main courtyard coming into view, with the large marble fountain and rows of slender trees lining the walkways.

"They're coming!" someone called.

Amy turned her head to see. Her heart dropped when she caught a glimpse of flashing armor and glinting spears. The queen's guards were flying in from all over the palace, closing in on them.

"Hurry!" Amy cried.

The fairies carrying her, though they were strong, were already laboring from her added weight and the strain of flying so fast. Still, they saw the pursuing palace guards and strove even harder, swooping toward the upper level of the palace, above the kitchen through which Amy had escaped earlier.

The topmost level of the palace wall contained many wide archways looking out onto the courtyard. The whole level glowed with warm light from within. As they flew higher on their approach, Amy could see colorful tapestries and smooth white columns.

The fairies landed, breathless, depositing Amy on a shiny marble floor and staggering forward away from the entrance.

Amy rushed farther into the room as well, though she had no idea where she was supposed to go. She hastily looked around to see if there was anywhere she might hide from their pursuers, and she realized that this was one of the biggest rooms that she had ever been in, with a high vaulted ceiling and shining golden motifs on white marble pillars. Royal-blue banners streamed from below stained-glass windows. Hundreds of blue sapphires sparkled from golden candelabras and a carved stone mural high above the throne.

She couldn't appreciate the beauty of the room for long, though. Seconds after her guards released her, dozens of palace guards caught up to them, swooping in between the support beams in the wall and wielding their crystal-tipped spears.

There was no talking, no hesitation. Their enemies burst in and started attacking immediately, shooting blindingly explosive spells from their spears or simply striking with their sharp-pointed spearheads. One second, the throne room had appeared to be a place of ancient and mysterious beauty. The next, it was a violent and bloody battle.

CHAPTER TWENTY-ONE

Amy stumbled farther into the room, away from the swinging spears and bursts of magical energy. Something came crashing down from the ceiling, shattering into hundreds of sharp shiny bits against the floor. She tripped over a hard chunk of bright gold and landed on a jagged piece of metal. It scraped against her arm, shooting hot pain through her skin.

"Amy, are you all right?"

It was Flax. He was crouched next to her and holding out a hand to help her up. Amy wasn't sure she wanted to get up yet. There were still explosions and shouting, and struggles were happening everywhere.

"Come on, let's go somewhere you won't get hurt." He grabbed her arm and pulled her along with him. She couldn't tell where they were going.

Finally, she was crouching behind a low wall with Flax gently pushing her back farther.

"I'm going to help my father. Stay here!"

What? Flax couldn't fight out there with all those powerful fairies. Amy gripped his arm to stop him. "Don't go out there! You'll get hurt!"

He put his hand over hers and softly pried away her fingers. "I can't sit by and do nothing!" he said.

Then he reached back and pulled the bandage from his wing. Gripping his talisman in his hands, he concentrated, and Amy saw the bent and damaged membrane straighten and heal before her eyes. Then Flax gave her shoulder an affectionate squeeze before turning and flying headlong into the fight.

Amy watched Flax go, but she quickly lost track of him in the violent, churning battle.

After a few moments, her eyes started to sting from some burning fumes and she had to keep blinking to clear her vision. It felt like someone had chopped a thousand juicy onions and filled the air with their irritating vapor.

Then she realized that the burning sensation might be a spell someone had cast to disable one side of the battle. If your enemies were blinded, surely they would be easier to defeat. And, for these fairies, if your enemy was forced to use their magic to be able to see, it would weaken them and also make them easier to subdue.

Amy rubbed her eyes, squeezing out burning tears. She wished she could make it stop. It seemed so unfair. If the palace guards were going to fight weak, recently released prisoners, they could at least do it on even ground.

She forced her eyes open, trying to see Flax and the princess among the milling fighters.

There she was! She was blocking aggressive spells from no fewer than five of the queen's guards hovering around her. They were staying back, seemingly hesitant to close in.

Princess Lily made a gesture with her hand and three of their spears flew into the air, impaling themselves deep in the ceiling. Two of the spear owners quailed in fear. One flew up to try to remove his spear where it was buried in the stone.

Amy looked around to see if she could spot Flax in the battle, feeling guilty for hiding behind a wall but not knowing what she could do to help her friend.

She found him. He'd somehow gotten his hands on a royal guard's spear and was whirling around fighting against an enemy twice his size. He was flying circles around the bigger fairy, shooting jabs of magic at him from the spear tip. He didn't seem to be doing much damage, but the guard was getting quite enraged.

Amy smiled and almost giggled at the sight, even though she was still terrified for her friend.

Then there was a booming noise and a flash of white light from outside. A contingent of armed fairy soldiers suddenly flew into the throne room to join the palace guards in battle. With them was Queen Orchid, looking furious and fierce as she wielded a slender scepter that looked too delicate to fight with.

Though it looked delicate, the queen's scepter was powerful. Fairy after fairy fell, immobile with just a touch of her magic. The tide had turned, and Amy's friends were fighting a losing battle.

"STOP!" Princess Lily's voice rang out suddenly.

Everyone froze.

Queen Orchid turned to look at the princess, but all the other fairies in the throne room were frozen in place, immobile in the middle of their battle poses. One guard was frozen with his spear poised to strike Zinnia in the face. A burst of blue-white magic energy hung motionless in the air on its way to collide with a pillar, having just missed its target. Several fairies were lying or curled on the marble floor among silvery pools of fairy blood.

Hovering in the air at an awkward angle, Flax was

frozen in the act of tumbling toward the ground, his wings broken again. The guard fairy he'd been tormenting was flying over him in grim victory, holding his spear in his hand, ready to strike.

The only ones not frozen were Queen Orchid and Princess Lily.

Amy watched as the queen turned to regard her sister with a cool stare. "Lily," she said, lifting her chin with an air of indignant superiority.

The princess hovered lower and landed among the paralyzed warriors to walk closer to the queen. "You know why we came here today, Orchid."

Orchid sniffed disdainfully. "You thought this would stop me?"

"Nothing else has. I've tried reasoning with you. I've tried showing you how important the doors are to fairy life in Titania. I've tried peaceably holding you back. But you refuse to be dissuaded. Force is the last option we have left. What else can I do?"

"You have been a nuisance to me for far too long. You should have stayed on the other side of the door with your precious human husband and out of my way."

"Orchid, please! I don't want to keep fighting, but I will if you force me. If you would just . . ." Lily stepped closer, pleading with her hands. They were within arms' reach of one another.

"No, this is it. We are ending this now. And you will not be able to stop me!" With a lightning-fast move that Amy almost missed, Queen Orchid reached out and grasped the princess by the throat.

Horrified, Amy thought the queen was going to strangle her. Instead, Queen Orchid wrapped her fingers around the shining golden chain of Princess Lily's talisman and ripped it off her neck.

The chain snapped.

Princess Lily screamed like she'd been stabbed through the heart.

In the same instant, the freezing spell that she'd cast broke and suddenly everyone was moving again like they didn't realize anything had happened, fighting and casting spells that shattered the air around them.

Ignoring the rest of the battle, Queen Orchid gestured toward her sister, throwing her across the room with a surge of magical power.

Lily hit the wall hard with a loud crack that Amy could hear even over the rest of the battle. Then, before anyone could react, a mound of clear crystal formed around the princess, like invisible water freezing to ice, encasing her and trapping her within.

Amy squeezed the top of the low wall with her hands, looking around at the other battling fairies. None of the ones on her side seemed to have noticed what was going on. Or, if they had, they weren't in a position to do anything about it. All around the throne room, pairs of fairies were locked in intense fighting. Amy noticed that the flashes of magical light and stone-shattering explosions were happening a lot less frequently. The fairies must be starting to run low on magic.

Her eyes were drawn to a small, dark-haired fairy writhing on the ground. With a jolt of horror, Amy realized that it was Flax. No longer strong enough to fight, he was trying to scoot himself away from the war raging over and around him. As she was looking at him, three fairies clashed together and crashed to the floor; one of their spears struck the floor next to Flax's head with a small shower of sparks. Flax cringed and rolled away. Amy noticed that he was holding his leg at an odd angle; one of his wings was also bent and two others were broken off.

Amy picked herself up and crouched at the end of the low wall. The fighting was fierce, but it didn't seem like any of the fairies were paying attention to her. She had to risk it. She couldn't sit back and watch Flax lying helpless on the ground and getting pulverized.

When the way seemed a little more clear, she rushed out from behind her hiding place and scrambled toward him. Chunks of marble littered the floor from spells shattering the ceiling and pillars. Injured fairies lay here and there, writhing in pain as Flax was or lying disturbingly still.

Amy tried to focus only on Flax. She tripped and slipped over the slick floor. A magical explosion burst next to her and she fell forward, catching herself with her hands before her face smashed into a chunk of broken ceiling resting on the floor. She noticed absently that her arm was bleeding, her red blood mixing with the silver fairy blood smeared everywhere around her.

She finally reached the area where Flax was; he was still trying to drag himself to safety.

"Flax! Come on!" She put her arms under his and started pulling him back toward the wall.

"Amy? What are you doing?" He gasped.

"I'm saving your skin again!" she growled through clenched teeth. "What does it look like?" She pulled harder, managing to slide him back several steps.

Flax groaned in pain as she tugged and dragged him the rest of the way across the floor, over rubble and broken crystal and through damp patches of fairy blood. She tried not to look too closely at what was happening all around them, focusing instead on the one task at hand, which was saving her friend.

When she finally got Flax mostly behind the low barrier, Amy crouched next to him, panting from the effort and shaking all over. "How bad are you hurt?"

"Pretty badly. Many others are worse off. With time and elixir, I would be fine." He sighed and closed his eyes, leaning his head against the wall.

"It's all over, isn't it?" Amy asked. "I haven't seen the door anywhere. She must have already destroyed it. And my mother . . ."

Flax shook his head. "It's over for us, but there is still some hope for you. The door is there, behind the throne." He tilted his chin toward the dais where the queen's throne sat. "The whole palace was built around it a thousand years ago, when the ancient fairy queen, Titania, used her magic to create a gateway to between the worlds."

Amy looked and saw the throne, shining and beautiful, carved so delicately it looked like it might fall apart if someone sat on it. Behind the throne, the back wall was decorated with two shining white trees. Their branches met at the peak of an arch centered behind the throne, and the space between their branches and trunks was dark, blacker black than any paint or fabric that Amy had ever seen. Then, in a rush of amazed understanding, she realized that it wasn't a black wall—it was empty. She was looking at the door between the worlds.

At the bottom of the steps leading up to the throne, Amy noticed a low pillar of light blue crystal. Within the translucent pillar shimmered galaxies of patterns, as though fairy dust and powdered gemstones had been poured into it when it was being formed.

Flax had mentioned this pillar once, Amy remembered.

Another fairy cried out in pain amidst clashes of spears. Amy couldn't help looking, and she saw, with a sinking feeling in her gut, that Bromeliad was clutching his chest and falling to the ground. Amy wished there was something she could do to help, but what could a human do to stop Queen Orchid when an army of fairies couldn't even stop her?

"Amy?" Flax touched her arm to get her attention and gazed at her with a small frown through his pain.

"Yeah?"

"I know you wanted to go home, but . . ."

Amy blinked. "But what?"

"But I don't think I'll be able to take you back to your door. I don't think we're going to make it out of this. The queen will destroy this door soon, and then you'll never make it back to your world."

Amy laid a hand on his shoulder. "Don't feel bad, Flax. You did your best. And you got me to the princess like you promised."

Flax shook his head and grimaced. "So, I was thinking . . ."

"What?"

"Maybe you could go through this door? I mean, I don't have enough magic to send you through, but you seem to be able to open doors. Maybe you could get through this one. And take this with you." He held out his hand, which was clasped around a shining gold chain and milky-white pendant. It was Princess Lily's talisman.

"Go through this door? The Titania Door?" Amy asked, reaching out to take the talisman from him. "How will that help?"

"Well, it won't take you home. It goes somewhere else—a place called Waterford—but at least you'd be in the human world. And this talisman holds a lot of magic. Since you're Princess Lily's daughter, you might be able to use the magic in the talisman to cure your father. Orchid wouldn't let Princess Lily have it back anyway, and none of us can use it. But you might be able to."

Amy held the talisman and looked across the room where her mother was trapped within the mound of clear crystal. "But . . ."

Flax tried to push himself up but winced in pain. His right leg was limp; maybe he'd broken it.

"Listen," he said with a gasp. "If you don't go now, you'll be stuck here forever. And it's a lot harder to get home from here in Titania than it is to get back to your grandmother from somewhere else in your world."

The fighting was starting to die down in the throne room. A handful of fierce Guardians were facing off against the last of the queen's royal guard. The queen herself was standing back to watch, facing away from Amy and Flax's hiding place.

Amy saw the fairies fighting with their last strength to defend what they believed was their only source of the elixir that kept them all alive.

Then she looked down at her mother's talisman. Flax said it contained magic—magic that she could use to cure her father—but what would happen to all these fairies if the last door was destroyed? Even if the Titania Door wasn't the last one, it wouldn't take long for the queen to discover Flax's secret door.

"I can't do that," she said to Flax.

"What?"

"What will happen to all of you if I leave now?"

"There's nothing we can do about that now."

Amy hesitated. If she was wrong about this . . .

"Amy, please!" Flax hissed urgently. "If you hurry, you can get through before she notices. You have to go before she destroys the door!"

Amy looked toward the low pedestal below the dais, next to the low wall where she and Flax were hiding.

The last of the Guardian fighters was standing off against three of the queen's guards now. The rest were watching grimly, ready to step in again if needed.

"I can't stand by and let this happen. I have to do something!"

Flax's eyes opened wider. He started to speak, but before he could try to convince her any more, Amy ran toward the pedestal at the foot of the dais with her mother's talisman in hand.

CHAPTER TWENTY-TWO

Flax had only mentioned this pedestal once in passing, but she remembered what he'd said. Royal fairies could place their talismans on it, and if it accepted the talisman, the pedestal would absorb it and that fairy would rule Titania. If it didn't accept the talisman, then it would be destroyed.

Either way, Amy wouldn't have her mother's talisman anymore—the talisman that her mother needed to perform the healing spell on Amy's father.

She'd be losing her last chance to save him.

Tears sprang to Amy's eyes as she stood over the pedestal. The smooth top surface was covered with intricate silvery designs. They looked like the silver ink her name was written in on the blue box where she'd found her necklace. In the middle of all the designs, connecting them all, was a shallow divot in the crystal surface, just big enough for the talisman to rest in.

Amy held the talisman out in her trembling hand, guiding it toward that divot. This was where it would be absorbed or destroyed, however it went. This is where she threw away any hope of saving her father.

At the last moment, Queen Orchid turned and saw Amy standing over the pedestal. The queen's face twisted with rage. She screamed, drew her arm back, and hurled a spell across the room at Amy. Like a ball of white-hot lightning, it sizzled through the air toward her.

Amy dropped to the ground to dodge the blow, but the spell hadn't been aimed at her. It was hurtling over her head, arcing over the dais and the throne, and disappeared into the silent empty blackness of the Titania Door.

The floor rumbled. The walls started to shudder. Dust and chunks of stone fell from the ceiling. Two of the supporting pillars in the outside wall broke apart and collapsed; cracks spread across the surface of those remaining.

Amy fell facedown on the ground, covering her head with her arms. She remembered what had happened the last time, when the queen had destroyed the door in the Crystal Cavern.

An ear-splitting crack shot through the room. The wall behind the throne collapsed as a shockwave rent the air around them, filling the throne room with a cloud of choking dust.

As the dust started to settle around her, Amy pushed herself up on her arms and looked around. Queen Orchid was watching her with a victorious smile on her face.

"Now it is done," she said. "I was planning to send you through first, human girl. You don't belong in our world. But now nothing you do can make any difference."

Amy stood weakly, bracing herself against the dust-covered pedestal. Her eyes met the queen's. The remaining guards were staggering to their feet, bruised and battered from the battle and the explosion of the door.

Then, without a word, before Queen Orchid could do anything else, Amy slapped her mother's talisman into the divot in the pedestal.

The pedestal reacted immediately. The whole thing glowed blue-white. The galaxies of gold flecks within swirled and aligned themselves with the markings on the surface. The talisman itself warmed to her touch and sank into the material of the pedestal.

Amy wasn't sure what any of this meant. Was it

working right? Would it not work at all because she was the one who'd put it there? Maybe only the rightful owner of a talisman could place it. In that case, maybe she'd made a drastic mistake.

"You foolish child! What have you done?" Orchid screamed from across the room. She sprinted over the rubble, dust, and fallen fairies toward Amy with a frantic look in her eyes.

Remembering how violent the spell was that destroyed the door behind her, and afraid of the queen's reaction, Amy ran over to Flax and crouched down behind the wall with him. He didn't say anything; he just looked at her in shock. His breath was coming shallowly and his face was starting to look slightly grey.

Queen Orchid didn't follow Amy. She didn't seem concerned with her at all anymore. She stood at the pedestal, trying to pry the talisman out. She spoke strange words over it, touched it carefully with her own talisman, and even tried casting the same destructive spell on the pedestal that she'd used on the door, but nothing she tried worked. The pedestal seemed completely impervious.

"Is it working? I can't tell," Amy whispered to Flax.

"I don't know. I've never seen this before," he whispered back.

Then, from the other end of the room where the

queen's guards stood stunned, the mound of crystal burst apart, crumbling into a pile of shiny clear stones.

Princess Lily fanned her wings to shake off the last of the flecks of crystal and stepped out of her prison, gazing around the room and taking in the situation. She saw the pile of rubble behind the throne and her eyes narrowed.

Amy peeked over the low wall to see what would happen.

Queen Orchid stood tall, staring down her sister as she approached. "It doesn't matter now. I've destroyed the last door. They're gone. You can't make the connection again now that they're all lost. We must learn to survive without the human world now."

Behind Orchid, the pedestal glowed brighter for a moment and sent a pulse out through the ground that made Amy's skin tingle. Then it dimmed to the same clear blue it had been before.

Lily held up her hands and looked at them with an awestruck expression on her face. Then she dropped her hands and seemed to notice Orchid for the first time since emerging from her prison. "Step down, Orchid. I am the rightful queen now."

"I tell you, it doesn't matter! You can be queen now all you like. Send me to prison or banish me to Dragon

Island. I've done what I intended to do. The doors are gone."

In the stress of the situation, Amy couldn't stop herself from laughing. "She still doesn't know about your door!" she hissed to Flax.

"What was that?" Orchid snapped, looking across at Amy and Flax with sudden ferocity.

Amy slapped her hand over her mouth. What a stupid mistake! After all this time, she had to go and give away the secret at the worst possible moment!

Orchid stalked toward them, raising her hand in a gesture that clearly indicated she was preparing a devastating spell.

Then she stopped, hand still raised, eyes still glaring, foot outstretched to take her next step.

"Orchid, I'm surprised at you," Lily said in a deceptively calm voice. "Is that any way to treat your favorite niece?"

Amy looked up at her mother in time to see the new queen flick her fingers casually. Orchid dropped to the ground, her eyelids fluttered closed, and she breathed softly in a deep enchanted sleep.

Amy started to climb out from behind the wall, but her mother turned to face the remaining royal guards who had fought so hard for Orchid just moments before.

The guards looked between Lily, Orchid's sleeping form, and the pedestal where Lily's talisman had disappeared. Then, almost in unison, the four of them knelt down before her and murmured, "Your Majesty," bowing their heads in respect.

The new queen approached and briefly laid a hand on each of their heads. Their injuries immediately started fading.

"I need you four to help me attend to the injured. Find those who need help the most urgently."

"Yes, Your Majesty," they answered and immediately fanned out to search among the fallen.

While they were looking for injured survivors, Queen Lily focused on the structure of the throne room. The battle had damaged supporting walls and pillars, leaving the whole place crumbling dangerously around them.

In an amazing display of power, Queen Lily used her magic to lift stones, fuse marble, and reverse large portions of the damage.

"There." She sighed, turning to face one of the guards approaching her. "Now it won't come crashing down on us."

Amy blinked. What was she doing? She was just sitting there in a daze while Flax was injured!

"I'll ask her to heal you," she said, rising from behind the wall.

But he grabbed her arm to stop her. "No, let her take care of the others first. Just sit here with me."

Amy hesitated uncertainly, then turned around and scooted next to Flax. He was leaning against the wall still, his broken wings crushed between his body and the smooth marble. He had grey bruises scattered over his face and arms. His right leg looked oddly deflated halfway between his knee and ankle.

"That was . . . a good plan," he gasped. "How did you know it would work?"

"I didn't," she admitted. "It was the only thing I could think of."

"But . . . your father."

"Don't worry. I knew that it meant she wouldn't be able to save him. But I couldn't stand by and let you all die." She looked down at her empty hands, still tingling from the magical radiance of the talisman when she'd put it in the pedestal. "He wouldn't want his life in exchange for yours."

Flax struggled to sit up better, but then he slid back against the wall with a groan.

Amy grabbed his shoulders and was helping him up when Queen Lily came around the corner and saw them. She looked a little tired from her efforts, but she knelt down in front of Flax and rested her hand on his head. Amy watched as all of his cuts sealed themselves, his bruises vanished, his leg grew straight and strong, and his wings spread out whole again.

Then, smiling softly, she rested her hand on Amy, and a familiar warm tingling sensation spread over the cuts and scrapes across Amy's arms. She hadn't even remembered she was hurt.

Queen Lily sighed and dropped her hand, standing to her feet.

Immediately, Flax jumped up and knelt before her. "Your Majesty, thank you."

She smiled at him, and then Zinnia and Bromeliad approached. "That is the last of them, Your Majesty," Bromeliad said. "We'll take the fallen out to the back garden for their families—"

"Yes, that will do," she interrupted. "See to it that the families and clans are notified as soon as possible. I have other business that must be attended to first. I will join you as soon as I can. And one more thing. Take my sister to the west tower. She won't wake soon, but if she does before I return, she must be contained until we can decide her fate."

The two guards nodded and turned to carry out their new queen's orders.

"Amaryllis, will you tell me what happened? I understand that my talisman passed Queen Titania's test and that my sister destroyed the door, but I don't know how any of this came to be."

"I did it," Amy said. "I put your talisman on the pedestal. Flax told me about it before, so I knew what the pedestal was for. But you were trapped and everyone was getting hurt, and I didn't know what else to do." She started to choke up and decided to stop talking before she started crying.

Queen Lily took Amy into her arms and embraced her. Her mother smelled like a blanket of wildflowers in a warm, sunny meadow. Amy hugged her back tightly as tears leaked out of her eyes.

When she opened her eyes again, she noticed that the sky showing through the archways in the wall was definitely lighter than it had been when they first came into the throne room. The sun was starting to rise.

Her mother released her and noticed where she was looking, following her gaze out to the brightening sky. "We'd better get you home then."

CHAPTER TWENTY-THREE

Amy, Flax, and Queen Lily stood together on the wide balcony outside the observatory. The sky in the eastern horizon was starting to glow pale blue with a hint of orange. A dark silhouette rose and soared toward the palace, growing larger every second until Amy could see what it was.

Broad feathered wings, shining like burning gold, beat powerfully through the air over sleek, muscular shoulders. The great beast clawed at the air with sharp talons as it approached, landing gracefully and lashing its long lion's tail as it approached Queen Lily.

"This is Sunblaze," she said, stroking the feathered neck of the gryphon. The creature had the front end of a golden eagle, complete with beak, wings, and talons, but the rear end of a powerful lion. "She's been my most reliable royal mount. And today, she will carry you back to the door to your home."

Amy slowly approached, remembering how skittish Thistle and Bracken had been at first.

"Don't be afraid; she is quite used to company. Even human company, but that's a story for another day." Lily laughed musically, then grew somber and sighed a small, sad sigh. "Here, allow me to help you to your seat."

"We rode white stags through the mountains on the way here," Amy said as her mother lifted her to Sunblaze's warm back. "They were nervous of me at first."

Lily paused and looked at Amy. "You rode one of the white stags of Mt. Oberon?"

"They're friends with Flax, and he asked them to help us."

Her mother's gaze turned to Flax. "Tell me about this. I know those stags from my own time in the mountains. They don't make friends easily."

Flax started telling the story as they flew into the sky over the parapet. Flax and Queen Lily went whirring straight up, but Sunblaze swooped down, picking up speed as she dropped toward the courtyard with her wings spread. Amy threw herself onto the feathered neck, holding on tightly as she had when riding Bracken. They gained altitude as Sunblaze made steady, deliberate beats of her wings, lifting them over the ramparts and out above the royal city.

As they leveled off, Lily and Flax rejoined her.

"I should have warned you about that," Queen Lily said. "Sunblaze can be a bit lazy. She prefers to glide whenever possible."

"Oh, it's . . . it's all right." Amy gasped, trying to release her stranglehold on the gryphon's neck in front of her. "Whatever works for her."

Sunblaze's powerful wing muscles were beating at the air steadily now, picking up even more speed. The wind whipped through Amy's hair, tugging out the last remaining flowers that Flax's mother had given her. The scenery passed under them, looking like a diorama of an artist's version of paradise.

"Amaryllis, there's something I need to make sure you understand," her mother said, speeding up to fly ahead of and above her and the gryphon. "I can't go to the human world now. Not now that my magic is tied to Titania. If I went through the door, I would lose all my magic and . . ."

She didn't finish that thought, but Amy understood. She'd seen what happens to fairies who lose their magic.

"So you can't save my father," Amy said. It wasn't a question. She'd known that's what she was giving up when she put her mother's talisman to the pedestal. Still, it tore at her heart to say it out loud.

"I'm afraid not," Lily answered.

They flew over the river at the foot of the mountain and Flax noticed the tree root bridge he'd made for them to cross over the water.

"I still don't know how I did that," he said, looking down at the vine-covered bridge.

Amy looked, too. She remembered watching it happen, the roots stretching out to join one another, like they knew exactly how to form a convenient walking surface and were happy to do so for them. They'd widened and thickened and sent down supports exactly as Amy had expected as she watched it happening.

"You made that bridge?" Queen Lily asked, looking at Flax in surprise.

"Well, yes. But I don't really know how I did it so well. I was only trying to get the roots to stretch over the water so we could hold on to them as we crossed. The water isn't too deep, but it's swift and would have washed us away. The trees seemed to almost want to form a whole bridge for us to cross instead. It surprised me."

Lily looked between Flax and Amy, then arced over Amy's head to fly between the two of them. "You said the stags trusted her?"

"Uh, yeah."

"Blood signature explains why she could unlock the door from her world and how she escaped the palace room. The magic is within the doors, not in her blood. But I don't understand how she opened the prison doors. It takes both authority and magic to drop the barriers there."

Flax rubbed the back of his neck and glanced at Amy with a shrug. Amy could understand his confusion; her mother seemed to be changing topics rapidly.

"And the stags . . . they trusted her almost immediately?"

"Yeah, that was a surprise to me, too. I thought it probably wouldn't work but was still worth a try. And they took to her right away. They must have recognized her as a member of the royal family."

Lily was shaking her head. "They recognized her as my daughter, of course, but they don't care about bloodlines or heritage. They care about a fairy's nature, which they can read through their magical ambiance."

Flax and Lily looked at each other and both turned to and stare at Amy with curious and amazed eyes as they started to descend between low forested hills.

"What? What are you saying?" Amy asked.

They looked at each other again before Lily

answered. "I'm not sure yet. Come, though. We're almost there."

It was a good thing, too. The whole sky was starting to glow with pre-dawn light.

They flew quickly over Lake Village, and Amy thought she recognized Flax's house in the big tree near the docks. Did anyone in this village know what had happened at the palace yet? She wished she could go talk to Marigold and see baby Acorn again and tell them everything that they'd done, that Hawthorne would soon be returning home to them, that the last door was safe now, and that Lily was the new queen.

They coasted low over the river, following the shining water upstream, and, moments later, Sunblaze's paws and claws were splashing in the shallow water on the bank by a large tree.

Amy wouldn't have recognized the place if Flax and her mother hadn't been with her. The bend in the river looked like any other. The tree was large, but there were several larger ones nearby. There seemed to be nothing about this place to indicate that it concealed one of the most powerful spells in Titania.

Amy slid off Sunblaze's back and patted her soft feathered neck. The gryphon gave a gentle squawk, then lashed her tail and turned to run down the bank, spreading her wings again to take off in a burst of rushing wind.

Amy watched the magnificent creature as she soared into the air. Then she turned to join Flax and her mother, who were standing near the tree already, speaking in low tones to one another.

"I think I should get home now," Amy said, looking up at the pale sky. Songbirds were starting to flutter and whistle in the trees above them.

Lily knelt down in front of Amy and looked her seriously in the eyes. "Amaryllis, when you were at your grandmother's house, did you happen to find a small box with your name on it?"

"Yes, I did. I have the necklace here." She drew the chain out from under her cloak and showed the pendant to her mother.

Queen Lily closed her eyes and took a deep breath. It looked like she was trying to stay calm. "May I hold it for a moment?"

Amy pulled the chain over her head and handed the necklace over to her mother. When it left her hands, she felt a strange sense of loss, like a chair she was sitting on suddenly had one of its legs taken away.

"Have you ever attempted to use magic?"

"I . . . don't think so. Why? Do you think I have magic?"

"Something strange happened during the battle in the throne room," Lily said, looking at Amy's necklace. "One of the opposing guards had cast a powerful blinding spell early on, making the eyes of everyone on our side burn and tear up so we couldn't see. She probably used up most of her magic to do it. None of my fighters were strong enough to counter it, even with your generous donation of elixir. But before I could cast my own spell, the enemy's spell was neutralized. I didn't know who had done it, but the magic felt familiar."

Amy remembered her stinging, watering eyes in the throne room. She remembered wishing it would go away, and then it had. Was that magic?

Queen Lily held Amy's necklace in her palm, looking at it curiously. Then suddenly the pendant started to glow. Faintly at first, then brighter and brighter until it was shining like a small sun and Amy had to shield her eyes from it. Then, all at once, the light vanished and the talisman looked ordinary again.

Amy tried to blink the dancing stars out of her eyes.

"I knew it!" Flax laughed.

Lily was smiling, her eyes dancing with joy, as she handed the talisman back to Amy.

"What does it mean?" Amy asked.

Her mother laughed, too, then snatched Amy up in a

delighted embrace. "It means," she half-sobbed into Amy's ear, "that you can heal your father yourself!"

"What?"

"Is she really powerful enough for that?" Flax asked.

"It seems that, at the moment, Amaryllis is the most powerful fairy in Titania." Her mother smiled down at her with her eyes sparkling.

"How?" Amy asked, breathless. "How do I do it?"

"Take your talisman to him. It isn't complicated. His body will know what to do; you just need to give it the power to conquer the illness. You may feel weak and tired afterwards, but you definitely have enough magic to do it."

"I thought she might have magic, but I can't believe she's so powerful! How is that possible?" Flax kept looking between Amy and Lily.

"She is my daughter, after all," Lily answered, looking down at Amy with pride. "Now, go back to your grandmother. Heal your father. And . . . tell him what you learned here."

"I will . . . Mother."

Queen Lily kissed her on the forehead, and Amy turned to walk back through the door.

The darkness seemed empty as she went under the thick root of the tree, but she held out her hand to feel her way ahead and soon found her fingertips brushing against a wooden door. She took the handle, gave it a push, and the door swung open easily.

Amy stepped through into the dreary, dusty old barn. Sunlight was starting to stream in through the cracks in the walls and the holes in the roof, making the swirling dust motes in the air shine.

Amy knew that her grandmother might be looking for her already, and her father was still desperately in need of help, but before she rushed off to the farmhouse, she went outside to the rowan tree and filled her skirt with berries. Then she went back to the door and poured them past the barrier, hoping that Flax would still be there to gather them.

As she closed the door, she thought she could hear the sound of Flax's delighted laugh coming from the other side.

CHAPTER TWENTY-FOUR

The sun was definitely up now. Bright yellow light streaked over the distant rolling hills. The air had a chill to it that made Amy shiver, and the tall grass in the field was soaked with early morning dew as she waded through it.

As she drew nearer to the farmhouse, she could hear Grandma Kerry calling out, her voice mixed in with the sounds of clucking chickens and lowing cows. Amy hurried to find her.

"I'm here!" she called, running around the corner of the house.

Grandma Kerry was wearing a robe over her pajamas, with gardening boots on her feet. She whirled around when she heard Amy's voice.

"Goodness gracious! Where on earth have you been?"

"I . . . I went for a walk," Amy lied, feeling guilty. "I'm sorry. Can we go visit my father? I want to see him right away."

"What? Already? It's too early to visit, and we wouldn't want to wake him up."

"But . . ."

"And we need to change. I don't know where you got that lovely dress, but you shouldn't be running around outside in it. You've gotten it all wet!"

Amy looked down at the dress Marigold had given her. It was so comfortable, she hadn't even remembered that she wasn't wearing her own nightgown. It had indeed gotten wet as she ran through the dewy field.

Her own nightgown and boots must still be at Flax's house with his mother.

Her grandmother made her change into dry clothes. Then Amy had to wait until breakfast was ready. She wasn't hungry, though. Her stomach was tight, and she was starting to feel sick with anxiety.

Since she was being forced to slow down, little doubts were starting to creep into her mind. She picked at her scrambled eggs with her fork and worried. What if she didn't have any magic here in the human world? Maybe her magic was tied to Titania, too? Or maybe her talisman only worked there? It didn't seem magical now. It looked like an ordinary piece of jewelry.

Finally, Grandma Kerry saw that Amy wouldn't be content until they were on their way. She put breakfast away and started grabbing her things to go. Amy jumped eagerly into the car, and Grandma Kerry started the drive to the hospital.

Amy couldn't seem to keep still the whole way there. She fidgeted in her seat and fiddled with her necklace. She hadn't managed to eat any breakfast, but if she had, she was sure it would have come back up again.

"I haven't had any calls since yesterday," Grandma Kerry said, noticing how nervous Amy was. "I'm sure your father is doing fine. He's probably sleeping still."

Amy only nodded, looking out through the windshield to see if she could spot the hospital in the distance.

When they finally arrived, Amy was trembling with anticipation. Her grandmother took her hand again as they walked through the parking lot and into the main lobby. There were a few news reporters milling about outside. Maybe they'd finally caught wind that Brandon Porter, the famous musician, was hospitalized here.

Amy stayed behind Grandma Kerry and hid her face, just in case one of them might recognize her. None of them did.

When they got upstairs, one of the nurses took Amy and her grandmother back to her father's room. He was weak and tired and seemed only half awake. He looked even worse than he had the previous day. Amy could hear the nurse whispering to Grandma Kerry that he wasn't doing well and might not be able to talk.

Amy ignored the nurse and approached the edge of the bed where her father was lying. It seemed to be a struggle for him to breathe at all.

Amy pulled out her talisman and held it tightly in her hands. She still wasn't sure how this was supposed to work. How had she done it in Titania?

"Amy?" her father whispered, turning his head slightly to look at her.

"Hi, Dad," she said, putting her hand on his arm. His skin felt hot to her touch.

"You look so much like your mother," he murmured. His eyes were glistening.

Amy held onto him, willing the sickness to leave him, longing for his lungs to heal and the fever to leave.

"I know I do," she whispered.

He looked at her silently.

"I met her. I went through the door and found my mother."

His eyes widened a little. "You did?"

Amy continued to hold onto him, willing him to get

better, willing everything that was wrong with him to go away. She quietly told him what her mother had said about why she'd left and why she couldn't come back.

After a little while, his eyes fluttered closed and he seemed to fall asleep, but Amy kept talking, telling him all about the struggle in Titania and Queen Orchid destroying the fairy doors and how her mother had become the new queen. She told him how her mother's magic was tied to Titania so she couldn't come back but that Amy was with him now, and she would do what she could to help him.

She continued talking and willing him to heal until her grandmother came back in and placed a hand on her shoulder.

Amy hadn't even realized that she'd left.

"We should go now, honey. Your father needs to sleep."

Amy looked into her father's face. He seemed to be resting easier now, his skin was less pale, his breathing wasn't as labored, and the uncomfortable expression on his face was gone.

Amy fell asleep in the car on the way back to the farmhouse, and when they arrived, she only woke long enough to crawl into her bed and fall asleep again.

The phone rang early the next morning and Grandma Kerry hurried to answer it.

Amy, who was sitting on the couch and reading one of her father's old adventure books, tried to listen in and hear what they were saying. She didn't catch much, but it sounded like the person on the other end said, "We still want to run some more tests, but in my opinion . . ." When Grandma Kerry hung up the phone, she was smiling and crying with relief.

They packed themselves into the car again for another trip to the hospital. This time, when they arrived, Amy's father was sitting up on his cot, happily eating his breakfast.

Amy ran to him with open arms. He laughed and hugged her back, kissing her hair.

"You're doing better!" she exclaimed.

"I'm not even coughing anymore; it's like magic!"

"Does that mean you can come home with us today?"

"Well, they still want to keep an eye on me," he said, "to make sure I'm really all better."

"Is there anything we can get for you?" Grandma Kerry asked.

"You know . . ." He thought for a moment. "There is. I could really use a good chicken sandwich. The stuff they call food here is only food in the most academic of definitions."

"Ahem."

They looked to the door, where one of the doctors was coming in.

"Sorry, Doctor Stevens, but it's true, you know."

"That's fair enough," Doctor Stevens conceded with a chuckle and a nod. "I just came in to get Mrs. Porter caught up on what we're looking at here."

"By all means. You and my mother can go talk about all the boring medical details. And while you're doing that, I'll get caught up with my daughter." He smiled at Amy.

Grandma Kerry and the doctor stepped out, and Amy's father motioned Amy closer.

"Hey there, little bug. How have you been?"

Amy gulped. "Me? What about you? Are you really better now?"

"It does seem that way. But the doctors don't understand it." He chuckled and felt his chest with his hands, as though making sure he was really breathing with his own lungs.

Then he looked at Amy with serious, hesitant eyes. "Listen, the other day . . . when you came to visit me . . ."

"Yeah?"

"I thought I heard you say some things, and I don't know what was real and what I was imagining."

Amy bit her lip. She wasn't sure how much she should tell him. If he didn't know that her mother was a fairy, would he not believe her? Would he think she was crazy?

"Why didn't I ever meet Mom's family?" she finally asked. It seemed best to figure out how much he knew to start with.

Her father blinked in surprise, raking a hand through his hair. He had an IV taped to his arm and the motion jostled it. He winced and lowered his hand back to the bed.

"Well, it's kind of a long story . . ."

"Do you know who her family is?" Amy pressed, looking down at her fingers as she fiddled with a corner of the hospital blanket.

Her father was quiet for a moment before answering. "Yes . . . yes, I do know who her family is. We haven't visited because . . . well, they live very far away."

"I know." She looked up.

Her father was staring at her, studying her expression carefully.

"They live in a land called Titania."

He swallowed but didn't answer.

"I went there. I met Mom." She pulled her talisman out so her father could see it. "She taught me how to use my fairy magic so I could heal you."

"You met your mother?" he gasped.

Amy looked up at him again and saw that he was smiling. She nodded mutely.

"She's all right?"

Amy couldn't help smiling broadly, too. She'd been so afraid he wouldn't believe her, but he knew! "Yes. She's been there all this time trying to protect the fairies. But she's the new queen now."

"And you really went there? That's amazing!" he shouted, throwing his arms around her and pulling her in for a hug so tight she could barely breathe. "You have to tell me all about it! Did you go through the secret barn door or did she make another? What was it like? Did you meet Marigold and Hawthorne?"

Amy wasn't nearly done telling her father about all the amazing things that had happened to her in Titania when Grandma Kerry and the doctor came back in.

Her father was released from the hospital the next morning and came home to Grandma Kerry's house with them.

That night they celebrated his miraculous recovery with a meal of all his favorite foods. He told the story of how he met and grew to love Amy's mother, and how she taught him to make beautiful music.

Grandma Kerry smiled when he called her a fairy and told how she'd enchanted him. Amy could tell that she thought her father was using poetic language, like he often did in the songs he wrote.

"But, Grandma, it's all real, you know. My mom really *is* a fairy," Amy insisted.

Grandma Kerry chuckled and shook her head indulgently, the way adults did when kids talked about the Easter Bunny and leprechauns.

Amy looked at her father, and he smiled and winked at her.

There was a light knock at the door.

"I'll get it," Amy's father said, standing from the table and taking his plate to the sink on his way to the door.

"I wish you'd believe us," Amy said to her grandma. "But I guess this is the kind of thing you have to see for yourself before you can believe it."

Her father was talking to someone at the door. His voice was high with surprise. He sounded excited.

"You can believe whatever you want to believe about your mother, dear. It's harmless." She patted Amy's hand. "I wonder who could be at the door. We hardly ever get visitors way out here."

She was getting up to see who it was when Amy's father came walking back, carrying an envelope of creamy white paper closed with a royal-blue wax seal. He was turning it over in his hands, examining it with a disbelieving expression.

CHAPTER TWENTY-FIVE

"Who was at the door?" Grandma Kerry asked.

"What's that?" Amy asked at the same time, looking at the paper.

"That was vicegerent Mallow," he mumbled, seeming dazed.

"What?" Grandma Kerry asked.

Amy's father didn't answer. He slid his thumb under the wax seal, breaking it, and unfolded the paper. When it opened up, Amy saw that the outside edges of the paper were dusted with silver and delicately cut into intricate designs, like shimmering lace or skeleton leaves.

He read the missive in silence for a moment, and his eyebrows lifted in renewed surprise.

"What does it say?" Amy asked.

"We've been invited to the dedication of the new Titania Door. What does that mean?"

"A new Titania Door? But it was destroyed," Amy said, and then a sudden realization hit her. "That must mean she can fix it!"

"Who can fix what? What is going on?" Grandma Kerry asked, looking between the two of them and the paper.

"I honestly don't know," Amy's father said, looking at Amy quizzically.

"But then . . . we're going to go there!" Amy gasped. "We're going to see Mom!"

"We are?" her father asked as Amy took the invitation from his hand and read it carefully.

It was written with the same silver starlight ink in the same flowing hand as the box in which she'd found her talisman. Amy could only assume her mother had written it herself. It clearly stated that the whole family was invited to attend the ceremony on the following morning.

"I've never been able to get through the door on my own before," her father said.

"What door? What are you two talking about?"

"The fairy door in your barn, Grandma! The last fairy door in the world, and we're all going through it!"

The following morning, Amy, her father, and her

grandmother began the short hike to the barn shortly after the cows were milked and the chickens were fed.

Dew still clung to the tall grass, sparkling in the yellow sunlight, and Amy could hear birds singing in the branches of the rowan tree over the barn.

They approached the rickety door to the barn. It still hung awkwardly by a single rusty hinge.

Amy grabbed the edge and tried to pull it open. The door creaked loudly and a shower of dust and wood splinters fell around her.

"Oh, I don't think this is such a good idea," Grandma Kerry muttered, drawing Amy away from the rickety door.

"But we have to get in there!" Amy protested.

"Here, just a sec." Her father motioned them to back farther away, then he lifted his foot and kicked the barn door hard.

A loud boom rumbled through the building. The wood cracked, and Amy's father fell to the damp ground with an *oof*.

"Are you all right, Brandon?" Grandma Kerry asked, helping him up.

He stood, brushing the dirt and grass off. "Yeah." He chuckled. "Nothing hurt but my pride."

Finally, all three of them grabbed the door and pulled together. The wood cracked ominously. More showers of splinters and dust fluttered to the ground, but they finally managed to open it wide enough for everyone to fit through.

They passed through the shadowy interior of the barn until they stood before the fairy door.

In the daylight, it looked a lot less magical and mysterious. It was just an arched wooden door in the wall of the barn. Amy could make out the symbols carved around the frame, but only barely.

"Is this the door you were talking about, dear?" Grandma Kerry asked.

Amy nodded.

"Why, that's just a side door we added when your father was young."

Amy looked up at her father.

"You said you can open it," he said, smiling with barely contained excitement. "Go on. Show me."

She reached out and grabbed the handle. This time, when she touched it, she noticed a subtle thrill in her fingers that shivered through the rest of her body.

She pulled the handle, and the wooden door silently swung open.

A rush of warm fragrant air blew into the barn, and with it came the sounds of exotic birdsong, happy voices, and rushing water.

"Oh my!" Grandma Kerry gasped, putting her hand to her throat.

As before, the barrier between the two worlds shimmered with golden light.

Amy stepped forward, reaching out to touch it, and felt her grandmother's hand tighten in hers.

"Are you sure . . .?" The old woman's voice trembled, and her eyes glistened as she gazed at the enchanted door. Next to her, Amy's father was looking at the veil of light with such joy and expectation that Amy thought his heart might burst.

"It's all right, Grandma. Hold my hand." Amy pulled her forward. She felt the barrier open up around her as she passed through, granting her access to Titania.

Amy stepped out from under the giant root of the towering tree onto the wide, flat stone. She scarcely recognized the bank by the river below her. Warm sunlight shone around a crowd of fairies, most of them dressed in blue and silver royal uniforms.

Three pure-white winged horses waited in their midst, ruffling their feathered pinions and shaking their manes. When Amy emerged, the three fairies closest to her stepped forward and bowed and curtseyed gallantly. She almost didn't recognize Zinnia until the strong and beautiful fairy spoke to her.

"Your Highness, we've come to escort you and your

family to the palace."

Amy's grandmother and father emerged from the tree behind her, looking all around with wide eyes.

"'*Your Highness?*' You mean *me*?" Amy asked, glancing around to see if she'd missed seeing a royal fairy somewhere nearby.

Zinnia smiled at her. "Of course. You are Her Majesty Queen Lily's daughter, Princess Amaryllis."

While Amy was still processing this, Zinnia led them to the winged horses, and attendants helped them mount their steeds. Amy's grandmother and father appeared to be beyond words. Grandma Kerry kept whispering, "Goodness gracious," under her breath as she looked around.

Amy caught her father's eye, and he smiled nervously at her as he settled into his soft leather saddle.

The flight to the palace took hardly any time at all. They soared over the mountain in nearly a straight line, only veering around the highest mountain peaks. As they neared Tuleris, the sky grew more and more crowded with fairies. In the daylight, their wings flashed with vibrant colors as they flew, making the whole sky sparkle around them.

The city itself stretched out like a vast, colorful forest below, with the palace shining like a white beacon at the center.

Their steeds steadied their wings and glided in a slow descending arc to land on a wide balcony near the throne room. A royal entourage awaited them. Beautiful fairy maidens were dressed in elegant gowns with soft wings folded gracefully against their backs. Royal guards in gleaming armor wore stern but joyful expressions on their beautiful faces. Two female fairies wearing pale yellow gowns carried silver trumpets at their sides. Two male fairies in bright blue tunics carried poles with rich, blue flags bearing the royal emblem, the silver tree, flashing in the sunlight.

As they dismounted, Amy saw her mother coming forward, wearing a blue-white gown and a sparkling jeweled circlet on her brow. Her red hair shone like fire in the sunlight. She was smiling with excited anticipation, but she wasn't looking at Amy.

Amy turned and saw her father, somewhat shaken and hair messy from the flight, step around his winged horse and spot her.

"Lily?" He gasped.

Queen Lily nodded and made a kind of choked, half-sob half-laugh sound, but somehow it still seemed elegant coming from her. Then she rushed forward, and Amy watched as her parents embraced and kissed for the first time since she was a baby.

The gate-opening ceremony would be held in the

throne room, of course, which Queen Lily had worked at repairing in the days following the battle. Much of the rubble had been cleared away, but the wall behind the throne was still in ruins.

The last time such a ceremony was performed was over a thousand years earlier. Fairies from all over Titania journeyed from their homes and villages to be near, even if there wasn't enough space in the throne room for all of them to witness it.

Amy and her grandmother and father, being Queen Lily's family, had seats reserved near the front of the room, and the eyes of most of the fairies present were on the humans as much as they were on the broken fairy door behind the throne.

"I wish I'd dressed better for the occasion," Grandma Kerry muttered, smoothing out her khaki pants. She'd been expecting to spend the morning running around outside playing pretend with her granddaughter, not attending a royal ceremony in a fairy palace.

"Hush! I want to listen," Amy's father said.

A group of fairies stood before the throne singing. It was a ballad about the history of Titania and the opening of the first door. Amy couldn't understand most of it, but even so, the music was so hauntingly beautiful that she could have listened forever.

When the song was over, the queen stepped down

from her throne and approached the pedestal. Amy remembered pressing her mother's talisman into that pedestal and how it had been absorbed into the translucent crystal, binding her mother's magic to Titania.

The queen placed her hand on the pedestal. A low thrumming reverberated through the floor of the throne room.

Then she hesitated. She looked back at the battered wall, then glanced over at Amy.

The fairies in the room waited silently, but Amy saw that their eyes were shifting between their new queen and her half-human daughter.

"Amaryllis, would you join me, please?" her mother called.

"M-me?" Amy squeaked.

Her mother smiled and nodded, eyes dancing. "Yes. I have an idea, but I need your help."

Shakily, Amy stood and wove her way past her grandmother and father and through more senior and respected fairies until she was out in the aisle and walking toward the pedestal and Queen Lily.

"What can I do?" she asked in a low voice that still carried through the whole room. She wondered if there was some sort of magic that made whoever spoke in the throne room be heard by everyone.

"Help me make the door," her mother said.

"I . . . I don't know how."

"You don't need to. I know how. I just want you to lend some of your magic to it. You see, Queen Titania made the first door with pure fairy magic. Since then, we fairies have only become more and more isolated from the natural world. But you are part human, and more powerful than you know. With your help, the magic supporting this door might help bridge the gap between human and fairy again."

Amy clenched her hands and glanced around the room nervously. What if she tried but messed it up? Would she curse all of Titania with her mistake?

Her mother smiled encouragingly, and Amy finally nodded, swallowing her fear.

They approached the dais together with the crowd murmuring in astonishment behind them. Queen Lily held out her hands, and the cracks in the stone rim of the door started sealing themselves up.

Amy held out her hands, too, copying her mother's posture. She tried to will the door to fix itself. She wasn't sure if she was doing it right or not—she couldn't feel anything happening.

Then a different kind of energy started to crackle through the air. Amy could feel it, like loud music that she couldn't hear but that vibrated through her body.

She aligned herself internally to it, going with the

flow, and pushed it even harder.

The silent vibration grew stronger and stronger. It was a wonder the whole room wasn't shaking with it. Amy felt some obscure energy quickly draining from her—she wouldn't be able to last much longer.

Then something snapped. The thrumming stopped. The room was silent. Amy dropped her hands and opened her eyes.

The carved white trees behind the throne were whole again! Within the frame of their branches, a dark shimmering curtain of magic showed that the fairy door was restored.

Behind Amy and her mother, the crowd exploded into cheering and shouts and song.

The queen and princess turned together to face them. Queen Lily appeared to be as tired as Amy felt, but she looked down at her daughter with a proud smile that made Amy's heart swell.

Amy grinned as she looked out into the cheering crowd. To her right, her grandmother and father were clapping and smiling together. She saw her grandmother wipe a tear from her eye.

To her left, she noticed a smaller figure cheering boisterously and more loudly than most of the others. It was Flax, surrounded by his family and beaming at Amy with a radiant smile on his face.

AFTERWORD

How did Flax end up in that barn? What was he thinking when Amy came poking around? What good is a fairy without magic anyway? Read Flax's side of the story in THE DOOR BETWEEN. Available for a limited time. Get your free copy here:

www.nadavenport.com/thedoorbetween

Thank you for reading THE LAST FAIRY DOOR. If you enjoyed this adventure, please leave a review. Reviews help other readers find books they might like, and they fill authors' lives with joy.

ALSO BY N. A. DAVENPORT

THE WEREWOLF MAX SERIES

Lost in the Graveyard

Werewolf Max and the Midnight Zombies

Werewolf Max and the Banshee Girl

Werewolf Max and the Monster War (Coming Soon)

Made in the USA
Columbia, SC
20 October 2020